The
Other Side
of Silence

Also by
Joseph L.S. Terrell

A TIME OF MUSIC, A TIME OF MAGIC

A NEUROTIC'S GUIDE TO SANE LIVING

The
Other Side
of Silence
The Asheville Summer

JOSEPH L.S. TERRELL

BellaRosaBooks

BellaRosaBooks

THE OTHER SIDE OF SILENCE
ISBN 978-1-933523-24-8

First Printed: November 2007

Library of Congress Control Number: 2007939748

Printed in the United States of America on acid-free paper.

Cover photograph by Dirck Harris – www.pbase.com/harry1

Book design by Bella Rosa Books

BellaRosaBooks and logo are trademarks of Bella Rosa Books

10   9   8   7   6   5   4   3   2   1

Dedicated to the memory of my wife, Faye, the first reader, and the first to fall in love with this story.

"If we had a keen vision and feeling of all ordinary human life, it would be like hearing the grass grow and the squirrel's heartbeat, and we should die of that roar which lies on the other side of silence."

—George Eliot, *Middlemarch*

Prologue
AN ECHO FAINTLY HEARD

Looking back on it through the slow-motion tumble of years, it seemed clear that everything that would ever happen to him happened the summer he lived in Asheville at the dragged-out end of the Depression and before the beginning of the Second World War. Perhaps everything that will happen comes every summer, in one form or another—the freedom and prison of loves, the minute and the overwhelming, the winning, losing, and growing. Even death comes every summer, as it did that year when he was a boy of ten.

When he thought about it later, Jonathan realized that much of what unfolded that summer really began the afternoon rain came across Clown Mountain and flooded the meadow. From that time on, events stood out in his mind as clearly as if made of something hard and shiny like steel and put in the sun for the whole world to see. Yet, much of it was so closely his very own, so secret, so silent from all around him, he doubted if he would ever tell anyone all of what he felt and saw and knew that summer.

And he discovered that by reading meaning into that one period of his life, by understanding and learning from one summer of his childhood, then much of the muffling numbness that surrounded him could be breathed away. By opening up the silence of the past, by stepping into that secret land, there he could find the pain of awareness, the peace and the joy, awaiting him.

Chapter One

He sat in the cool late-afternoon shadows of Aunt Eva's front porch, his arms wrapped around his bare knees, and stared across narrow concrete Mattaskeet Road and the flat green meadow to the mountains, where roiling, dark thunderclouds grew larger and larger. After a few moments he cocked his head and listened, glancing around, puzzled.

The soft whirring of insects had stopped. The air was still.

He had come around from the backyard to be by himself on the porch. But now that it had started getting cloudy and quiet, Jonathan wasn't certain he liked being alone. He thought about returning to the side of the house where his brother and sister and two cousins played, but instead he sat hunched over on the wide, gray-painted boards of the porch, hugging his knees. He watched the almost-black clouds as they bumped into each other at the top of Clown Mountain.

Jonathan and the others had given the mountain

its name on a spring evening six weeks earlier, shortly after his family had to come to Asheville to live with Aunt Eva and Uncle Roy because of the Depression. They had been playing outside on the long, sloping front lawn, with its thick grass and large evergreens, and Jonathan had looked across the meadow to the mountain directly in front of them. He pointed to the odd-shaped tree that stood out at the top above the others.

"A clown," he said. "That tree at the top of the mountain looks like a clown in a long baggy coat." So they had named the small mountain, one of several that encircled them as if they were in a bowl, Clown Mountain.

Jonathan now wished they had named it something else because clowns didn't seem funny at all to him. Instead, the tree at the top of the hill looked monstrous and scary.

He watched as wind from the gathering storm swayed the clown tree back and forth and made it appear as if it laughed at some private joke. Jonathan didn't like that. But something else that afternoon nudged him toward an uneasy feeling.

Across the meadow at the foot of Clown Mountain, about a quarter of a mile away, the rickety Dennihan frame house squatted on grassless, trash-littered ground. A pigpen attached itself to the house so that to Jonathan the house and pen seemed to be one and the same.

The unpainted house appeared dark and still under the shadows of the heavy, swirling clouds. He wrinkled his nose as if he could smell the house and a dampness all about it. The house made him feel strangely afraid and sad at the same time, as if there was something bad about it. He was drawn to staring at the house in the same way that when they walked past the cemetery he glanced at the tombstones, even when he didn't really want to.

As if the clouds ripped open against the top of Clown Mountain, it began to rain. The curtain of rainwater moved from the top of the mountain, down its side to the Dennihan pigpen house and to Mattaskeet Creek that meandered through the meadow. The blinding sheet of rainfall moved quickly up to Mattaskeet Road in front of Aunt Eva's house and he could smell the cold falling water on the hot grass. The clouds looked as if they would never stop emptying out the rain.

Moments after the downpour swept across Aunt Eva's house, Jonathan's older brother, David, and their eight-year-old sister, Ellen, scurried around from the side yard to get out of the heavy shower and to watch the storm. They laughed, the rain splashing them as they ran.

"Wow!" David said, darting onto the porch. "It's raining just like it did in 'Hurricane,'" referring to a movie they had seen. He was always comparing things to either a movie or a radio program. David rubbed his hands across his head, flicking off droplets of moisture. "Those are the biggest raindrops I've ever seen. They're like marbles."

"Look at me," Ellen said. "How wet I got so quick." Her face glistened with wet and she grinned happily up at Jonathan.

Their two cousins had ducked inside the back-door of the house just before the rain started, not the kind who would enjoy being caught in the rain. He, David, and Ellen would deliberately get themselves caught in a downpour, just to add a little extra excitement, a bit more drama to things. His cousins would, as Aunt Eva said, be more sensible.

An hour later it was still raining as if it would never stop. They watched the meadow, which was hazy in the rain, fill with brown, fast-moving water from flooding Mattaskeet Creek.

That evening when Uncle Roy came home from his Pack Square law office, he talked about flash floods and some small bridge being almost under water. It rained all day, and into the evening until finally the rain stopped. Not until nightfall did the weather clear and the stars come out.

Jonathan went to bed thinking of how powerful and frightening the flood water seemed. Once, at the edge of sleep, he jumped as if he was falling and slid into a dream. He saw the tree at the top of Clown Mountain swaying back and forth laughing at something and then the clown tree pointed at the rickety Dennihan house. It was as if he was flying across the meadow, zooming headlong toward the pigpen house. Terrified, he sat up with a start and made a noise in his throat.

Sleepily from the next bed, David asked, "What's matter with you? You chasing a rabbit or something?" This is what they said that Jonathan's dog was doing when the dog jumped in his sleep.

"No . . . nothing," Jonathan mumbled. His heart

beat fast as he lay back down. He kept his eyes open for a while but they began to close and he drifted back to sleep and he did not dream anymore.

Chapter Two

The morning came sunny and warm and full of promise.

Before breakfast, Jonathan and David stood out in the front yard and peered across Mattaskeet Road at the meadow and the creek. The water had subsided in the meadow. Without really being able to tell in what way, Jonathan knew that the flood had changed the meadow and Mattaskeet Creek.

Later that morning Ellen came out to stand with Jonathan and David. As they stood at the foot of the porch's steps, Jonathan heard the front door open.

Their cousin Till said, "What are you all looking at?" She was almost thirteen, and as tall as David. She had been in the library practicing the piano—thirty minutes in the morning and thirty minutes in the afternoon. Aunt Eva saw to that.

Jonathan pointed toward the creek. "It looks different."

"I guess so. It got flooded." Cortland, Till's younger brother, came out right behind her. Jonathan knew Cortland had been lying on the sofa in the living room reading one of the many books Aunt Eva bought for him.

"Too wet to go down there now," Till said.

"Be okay this afternoon," Jonathan said, more to Cortland than to Till.

At lunch, Aunt Eva—who had taught school, Jonathan guessed, at least a hundred years before she finally "interrupted my career" to have Till and Cortland—chided Jonathan in her quiet, gentle but school-teacher way for being what she called picky with his food. He said, "Yes . . . ma'am," and kept his eyes fixed on his plate. Lunch had consisted mostly of green peas and carrots from supper the night before, along with warmed over biscuits and cold ham.

As soon as they finished eating, David led the way to, as he said, "Explore the havoc wreaked upon the land by flood waters," sounding for all the world like one of the radio announcers.

Till laughed her funny laugh that she saved for when David did something, but Jonathan said, "For goodness sakes, what're you trying to sound like? Here comes Don Winslow of the Navy?" He, himself, tried to sound like the announcer for the "Don Winslow of the Navy" radio program. But he couldn't get his voice pitched right.

Crossing Mattaskeet Road, which carried very little traffic that far out from town (due partly to the Depression, Uncle Roy said), they walked gingerly through the meadow. The ground was still sticky in places and matted with clumps of weeds that had been wadded together by the water.

Jonathan, who had been walking with his head down, said, mostly to himself and to Ellen, "I'm not a bit pickier with my food than Cortland is. Everybody's all the time saying I'm picky but they never say he's picky, too. That's because he eats a lot. But he's picky about what he eats."

Ellen solemnly nodded her support. "That's the truth," she said.

They studied the way the flood water had twisted weeds and sticks around the meadow. Jonathan saw a soggy dead mouse. He showed it to David, who poked at it with a stick. David bent down as if to pick up the mouse by its tail, but then drew his hand back and they kept walking toward Mattaskeet Creek, less than two hundred yards from the road.

When they got to the creek, Jonathan saw that the force of the water the night before had jammed a large log diagonally across the creek several yards below where the creek made a sharp turn at the roots of a maple tree. The log, swollen and bent at a slight angle in the middle, partially blocked the water and made a deeper pool by the thick roots of the maple. At its widest, the creek normally was ten feet across and two to three feet deep.

But the log had already enlarged and deepened Mattaskeet Creek somewhat at that point. The naturalness of what the log had done struck Jonathan and the others at almost the same time:

They decided to finish what the rain had started and make their own private swimming hole.

They shrieked with joy at the idea. "I'll bet nobody in the whole place around anywhere near here has a swimming pool like we'll have," Till said.

"We can have picnics and everything here," Cortland said.

"We want it for swimming, Cortland, not eating," Jonathan said. But then he thought about it a moment. "I guess we could bring some apples and biscuits and stuff down here if we got hungry swimming."

"This is no time for talk," David said like he was on the radio. "This calls for action."

They spent the early part of the afternoon carrying rocks larger than cantaloupes, struggling and grunting, backing up the log with them. Then David had the idea of filling burlap bags, or "toe sacks" as they called them, with sand and gravel and using these to finish the dam. Jonathan and the others knew where some of the bags were stored.

Uncle Roy got feed for the cow and chickens in the bags. When he emptied the bags, he folded them neatly into a corner of a shed behind the garage. Jonathan had never seen Uncle Roy use the bags for anything after they were folded and put in the shed. The stack of bags stood several feet high.

They half-ran back across the pasture toward the house, chattering about their project as they rushed into the kitchen, expecting to see Aunt Eva. Jonathan smelled black-eyed peas cooking and also something with onions in it. He liked black-eyed peas and onions, and it made him feel good to smell food being cooked. It was as if there was element of safety about it; when you were cooking you weren't going to have to move, or your mother and father weren't having disturbing conversations about finances. Things were going to stay the same for a while.

They scurried toward the front of the house, to find Aunt Eva. She sat in Uncle Roy's chair in the library, her glasses, which were secured around her neck with a narrow ribbon, pushed down on her nose. She held a book in her lap. Jonathan noticed she always read dull-looking books with no pictures or drawings, always minus the dust jacket, and with pages that had long ago lost any sheen they might have had. Her constant companions, the green package of Lucky Strike cigarettes with the bull's-eye and the nicotine-darkened carved ivory cigarette holder, lay in the ash tray beside Uncle Roy's rack of pipes and the humidor with the small shriveled apple in it. Jonathan thought the mahogany-colored apple resembled a mummy's head.

Aunt Eva smiled and told them to slow down and explain it again. With David and Till doing most of the talking, but Cortland butting in every so often, they told her about how the rain had moved the log, and the rocks they had carried, and how now they needed the toe sacks to completely finish their swimming hole and have the best one in practically the whole world. Aunt Eva hesitated, then smiled again and said not to take too many and to leave the stack orderly.

Jonathan knew that she spoke often of orderliness as one of the great goals of life. She lauded orderly compositions from her students, she said, and she believed in orderly personal business affairs, meals and an orderly ritual in bathing and getting ready for bed at night.

Jonathan told David that he didn't see how in the world their father and Aunt Eva could be brother and sister—not two people that different from each other.

But David said, "I don't know. Look at me and you."

And Jonathan did not know what to say to that, because it was true: David was tall for his age and slender and Jonathan and Ellen were of a shorter, stockier mold, like their mother's people. David liked to run things and get things organized; as for Jonathan, he really preferred to watch for a bit and decide whether he wanted to join in or not. Also, Jonathan was fully aware that because of David's dark curly hair that ringed his face and large eyes— which contrasted sharply with Jonathan's and Ellen's ruddier complexion and blond hair—grown-ups were all the time calling David "angelic."

Jonathan knew that was just plain not so, that David was anything but angelic and Jonathan got tired of getting the blame for things every time he turned around that were really David's idea to start with. Just one for instance would have been the time that David talked him into sassing the little girl who lived next to them in Athens and suggesting things to her that he knew he had no business suggesting; and then the girl told her mother who told their mother and Jonathan got fussed at about it when in fact it was David who put him up to it.

And David just sat back looking angelic and like he didn't know diddledy-squat about what was going on.

Thinking about that, Jonathan was about half-way mad as they hurried out to the shed behind the garage.

As they stepped inside, Jonathan felt the warmth of the closed-up wooden shed; the heat made the sacks give off their smell of feed and rough burlap. Jonathan forgot completely about being sort of angry as soon as they got in the shed and got busy. David said they would take six and he carefully counted them off. Jonathan said they might as well take seven to be sure. Then Till said she thought they should get one more to make it an even eight.

They carried the bags back to the creek, with Cortland and Ellen taking turns carrying the sturdy, short-handled shovel to load sand and gravel into the sacks. They could fill the sacks less than half full of wet sand and gravel and still tug them into place. They struggled the sacks onto one another at their growing dam. After getting a sack in place, Jonathan brought from the edge of the creek bed a few more shovels of wet gravel to let slide into the mouth of the sack, held open by Ellen or Cortland.

They were all soaking wet. Ellen worked at Jonathan's side much of the time, smiling up at him frequently as if to say isn't this wonderful? He was serious and business-like about the work.

The water in the swift-moving creek quickly responded. By late that afternoon they had a swimming hole large enough for the five of them. At its widest point, it was now about fifteen feet across, and at its deepest, near the base of the maple tree, the water reached Jonathan's shoulders.

Till, who Jonathan thought was in many ways bossier than David, decided that they would all christen the swimming hole formally the next morning, in some fashion she had not yet decided upon. They sprawled out on the grass near the bank of the swimming hole, tossing pebbles into the water and grinning proudly at each other about the dam they had built and their swimming hole.

Jonathan could tell by the sun touching the mountains and the long, darkening shadows that it was getting close to time to go back home. Always late in the afternoon like this, he knew he could hear distant sounds more clearly, as if each sound were all alone by itself. Just before dusk one evening he had watched Uncle Roy's cow from afar and could hear her cowbell sharp and clear when she shook May flies away from her face.

Once when he was standing in the church yard up Mattaskeet Road toward Asheville he gazed far across the road to watch the tiny figure of a man chopping wood on a hill behind Charnock's Store. Everything was still and quiet. The man's ax would come down silently, and then the sound of the ax hitting the wood came to Jonathan just as the man started to raise his ax. Jonathan had watched until the grownups and others with him started talking and he couldn't hear the man's ax, even when he started to raise it.

Jonathan thought about this as he sat there in the peacefulness of the afternoon and listened to the talk about what a great time they would have with their swimming hole and everything else during the summer that stretched before them.

It was just about then, after some mention had already been made about it being time to go back across the meadow and Mattaskeet Road to Aunt Eva's house, that David nodded solemnly toward the opposite bank of the creek and downstream. "Over there," he said. "Hubert."

Hubert, red-headed Hubert Dennihan, a boy close to Jonathan's age, though smaller, half crouched in the bushes below them and across the creek. He wore a pair of bib overalls, faded and too small even for his bony, sun-bleached and freckled body, and no shirt nor shoes.

When Hubert knew they saw him, it appeared to Jonathan that Hubert might try to smile at them.

But then Till yelled, "What are you doing there? Huh? What're you spying at us for?"

Hubert straightened up, hesitated a moment— and in that moment Jonathan thought about yelling out to Hubert that it was all right, but he didn't— and then Hubert turned and ran and it was too late for Jonathan to call out anyway, even if he really and truly had wanted to.

Jonathan watched the back of Hubert's red head, bobbing and jerking as he ran. He sat there and watched after Hubert, watched him disappear in the slope before the uphill course of the raggedy dirt road that led up the small moun-tainside to the pigpen house he lived in with his mother and father.

Hubert's father, darkly red-faced Albert Dennihan, was forever carting stinking barrels of slop in his rattle-trap of a pickup truck for the few hogs they owned; this lent weight to Jonathan's idea that somehow the pigs and the Dennihans were all one family.

The first time Jonathan saw Albert Dennihan— he had driven up in his loud, rattling pickup truck to Aunt Eva's to repay part of a three dollar loan—he was frightened by him. It was nothing Dennihan did as he stood at the back door. It was just the dark, glowering face that would break out in a smile that had nothing to do with the rest of his face or his eyes. As he talked with Aunt Eva, showing large stained teeth, he promised more of a payment later and she assured him they trusted him.

Jonathan could smell the hogs and garbage and whiskey. He wondered why both his aunt and uncle were so polite to Mr. Dennihan and so tolerant, and guessed it was because Mr. Dennihan was the only one around who could do some of the chores, like cleaning out the cow stable, that Uncle Roy wanted doing from time to time. But maybe, too, his aunt and uncle felt sorry for the Dennihans.

Aunt Eva had told Jonathan's mother, "Albert Dennihan is just one of those men who, Depression or not, would be down on his luck. Just one of those people for whom nothing ever really goes right."

When Aunt Eva had said that about being down on his luck, Jonathan had thought of his own father and wondered if she meant him, too, and it immediately had made him ashamed that he had thought of his own father in Dennihan's place.

David stood up, glanced toward the reappeared and miniature figure of Hubert climbing the road to his pigpen house and said, "Guess we'd better go on home."

Till stood, too, and stretched, brushed back her hair and muttered something about Hubert spying on them like a little sneak. She threw a rock into the water.

They turned and began to walk back across the meadow toward Aunt Eva's large gray stucco and stone house across the road. Jonathan peered over his shoulder toward the pigpen house. For a moment he paused to see whether he could see Hubert, perhaps watching them as they walked away.

He thought that for just an instant he saw a figure in the shadows by the edge of the house and the pigpen. But then it was gone. Jonathan looked up beyond the house and he could see the tree at the top of Clown Mountain waving back and forth.

He turned and started walking again, quickly catching up with the others, although he and Ellen usually lagged slightly behind. He felt a bit sad. He knew his feeling had something to do with the Dennihans. In some dark and depressing way Jonathan was afraid the Dennihans would be very much with them that summer. But he forced himself not to think of that, or feel that, so he studied the ground carefully as they walked.

Chapter Three

The sun had dried the ground considerably, and in some places the dirt cracked under the heat of the day. Using his bare toes carefully, Jonathan could kick up puffs of dust from the tops of small dirt clods. Ellen saw him doing this and she kicked at the dirt, too.

He and Ellen trudged a few yards behind David, Till, and Cortland. Although Cortland was closer to Jonathan's age, he usually walked along with his sister.

Ellen stopped kicking at the dirt. "We going to walk down to meet Mother?"

"Sure, I guess so," Jonathan said. He had been thinking about Hubert Dennihan. Then in a louder voice, he said, "David, you going down to meet Mother?" David did not answer right away so he asked him again.

"Maybe. I don't know yet," David said.

"We'll go, won't we?" Ellen said.

"Yeah," he said and nodded. Since their mother

had started working in town at an antique shop, Jonathan and Ellen almost always walked the three-quarters of a mile along Mattaskeet Road to meet her late afternoon bus. The antique shop also sold the china-head dolls their mother dressed in Civil War period clothes she sewed by hand and on her Singer sewing machine. They had the sewing machine shipped by Railway Express from Georgia to Asheville. She got the job when she took three of the dolls with her and rode the bus into town to Schwartz's Antique Shop. She asked Mr. Schwartz fifty cents apiece for the dolls. He gave her sixty cents each and offered her a job, part-time. He said he wanted her to understand he might not be able to keep her on because of the Depression. But he wanted her to bring more dolls to sell, which thrilled their mother because she loved to dress the dolls and would work by the hour on them while listening to the radio.

Occasionally their mother would get a ride home with Uncle Roy, but he almost always stayed at his Pack Square law office until six, and Jonathan's mother was usually stepping lightly off the bus shortly after five-thirty, smiling at them standing by the edge of the road waiting for her where the bus turned around at the end of its run.

As he thought about his mother working, Jonathan's mind slipped to why they were here in the first place. For more than a year in Georgia, their father, Joel Clayton, had tried to keep the soft-drink bottling business going. But he was having a harder and harder time meeting payrolls, buying supplies and keeping the trucks on the road. When the business failed, there was no where else to go but to his sister's. Their mother and father had sat up late at night talking. Jonathan had heard them several times, and he cried.

David said to him, "It's not so bad. Lots of people are going out of business because of the Depression."

But it was more than the business failing and Jonathan could not make David see that it was the unhappiness and the sadness in their father's eyes and the way he walked so slowly and a whole lot more that Jonathan had trouble putting into words. It was the change, the change to sadness, that made Jonathan cry, knowing somehow that something had ended and he was afraid it would never be the same.

When their father brought the family to his sister Eva's house in March, he had tried desperately to find work around Asheville. When, week after week, he had no luck, he decided to go to Washington, where there were supposed to be government jobs available. It was then, in early May, that their mother had started working in town.

After they had started to a country school near Aunt Eva's, a school Jonathan hated, a different feeling that he did not like—was it really embarrassment and a touch of shame?—began to creep in and Jonathan would push it out of his mind because he did not want to be ashamed of his father. He did not want his father to be out trying to find a job and coming home and not having one.

When they got to the edge of the road, Ellen

broke the silence by asking again about going to meet their mother.

Jonathan said, "I've told you at least a dozen times that we're going to meet her. Now hush up about it."

Ellen got a hurt look on her face but she didn't say anything.

Jonathan felt bad about snapping at Ellen, but he had been thinking about Atlanta and how raw cold it had been in the big old house there that winter and about his father going to Washington to try for a job and his mother working and he had to be cross with someone.

They started up toward the house through the tall, loose evergreen hedge at the beginning of the yard. Going around the west side of the house, away from the driveway, they went to the large screened-in back porch, with its old smells of light lubricating oil, apples and a damp clothes basket. An oval wicker basket of aged clothes pins rested in its place on top of a long-unused pedal sewing machine.

In the kitchen, Aunt Eva, wearing a gray striped cotton apron, stood by the sink in the large square kitchen. She turned as they came trooping in. "Well, well, the reappearance of the little brood, and all looking like half-drowned rats," she said in her polished, clear school-teacher voice.

Cortland peered at the sink and then at the table. "Can we have . . . may we have something to eat?"

"Not yet, dear. It's almost five-thirty. We'll be eating in an hour."

"Nothing? We're starving. We've been building a dam and everything."

"Well, a half an apple apiece."

"It won't come out even," Cortland said. "I'll just eat a whole one."

"We'll just save the other half," Aunt Eva said. She cut the apples and wrapped one of the halves carefully in wax paper and put it in the refrigerator.

"Is it time to meet Mother?" Ellen asked.

Aunt Eva patted Ellen's thick blonde hair and nodded. "It's just a little more than ten minutes before her bus. She called and said she wasn't waiting for Roy."

To Jonathan, Aunt Eva said, "You're going with Ellen, of course."

"Yes, I guess so. Yes, ma'am."

"Run along and be careful. There's getting to be more and more traffic now-a-days . . . in recent months," she added, correcting herself as she frequently did, as if she were writing a composition.

As for the road, however, to Jonathan it almost always seemed deserted.

Aunt Eva spoke again as Ellen and Jonathan started out the door to the back porch, her voice, though light and cheerful, touched with seriousness: "Better be careful, too, because I haven't heard Mr. Dennihan's truck and you know how he can drive, especially . . . sometimes."

Jonathan and Ellen went to the back steps and picked up their blue, rubber-wheeled iron toy tractors. The tractors had strings attached and the end of the string tied to short sticks. Jonathan held his

tractor by the stick and pulled it bumping and
spinning at the end of its string. This helped give it
the scarred and beat up appearance that he liked.
Ellen carried her tractor carefully in her hand.

Jonathan's dog Nobody pranced eagerly inside
the fenced area where the horse used to stay.
Jonathan had named his dog Nobody the year
before when they found him not even weaned in a
field near Atlanta. The mother dog, frightened and
half-wild, had abandoned the puppy as they
approached.

The dog could easily get out of the fenced-in
area but he knew enough to stay inside until
Jonathan and the others were out of sight, then he
would go wherever he pleased, frequently going
back inside the fence, pretending he had stayed there
the whole time. Jonathan knew better, and he had
half expected to see Nobody show up at the creek
when they were building the dam.

"Come on, Nobody," he said and the dog
twitched with happiness. During the spring he had
grown almost as large as a small German shepherd.
He was light colored and short-haired and had a
broad chest like a boxer.

The driveway was long and steep and rocky.
When they reached the road, Ellen set her tractor
down carefully; with his bare toes, Jonathan turned
his over on its wheels. They started up the white
concrete road, glancing back every step or two to
watch the tractors bouncing along on their rubber
wheels.

If he and Ellen played for long periods on the

concrete road they came home with their feet worn pink on the bottom.

Just beyond their uncle's acreage a vacant field adjoined a large cemetery, Memorial Garden, with great expanses of expertly trimmed green lawn. The owner had talked about allowing no more tombstones, Uncle Roy reported. The owner said tombstones marred the landscape, and in their stead, only brass plaques of identification fit flush against the earth to show where the bodies were laid out in neat, orderly rows. The owner said this was the modern approach to cemeteries and he promised to have his men keep the brass plaques polished so mourners could read the names easily. When he heard his uncle talking about this, Jonathan wondered if everyone in Asheville—except the Dennihans—was trying to make everything in the whole world neat and orderly.

Ellen glanced at the cemetery and back at Jonathan.

"I don't like it," she said.

He saw the rising hill of the cemetery. "It's not so bad in the daytime." He turned his eyes away.

"It's when it rains," she said, "and you can see it from Mother's room, and on Sundays. Of course at night."

"I don't pay any attention," he said and knew he was not telling the truth.

After a pause, Ellen said, "I wonder what happens when you die. I mean really happens."

"Heaven," he said, trying to believe it. "What in the world you doing talking about all this sort of stuff for anyway? Just hush up about cemeteries and dying and everything."

"Okay," Ellen said agreeably.

All five of the children had been to the cemetery a few evenings, at David's suggestion, to tell ghost stories.

Jonathan and Ellen had left early the last time, before it got dark. Uncle Roy had chuckled when Jonathan and Ellen came into the brightly lit kitchen. It seemed to Jonathan that Uncle Roy rarely laughed or even smiled completely and the chuckling made Jonathan even more embarrassed. Uncle Roy, a Republican former city judge, was one who still passed judgment in Jonathan's eyes. Ridicule from him, no matter how gently applied, was a sentence.

Just then a car appeared around one of the curves. Jonathan had forgotten Nobody until the car was near and Nobody darted toward it with a loud bark just as Jonathan tried to grab him. The driver eased toward the middle of the road to stay away from Nobody, although the dog nimbly swung around close to the front wheel, snapping at it and chasing the car for a few long powerful strides.

Jonathan called sharply after Nobody and smacked at the dog's hindquarters when he got him back. "Stop doing that, Nobody!"

The dog, panting, always seemed to be grinning mischievously when his mouth was open.

"You bad dog!" Ellen said. "You want to get yourself killed or something like that?"

Nobody looked contrite for just a moment but

then began to dance around with the attention he was getting and grin at them.

"Come on, stupid dog," Jonathan muttered and the continued toward the bus stop.

"Mother said you aren't supposed to call anybody stupid," Ellen said.

"I wasn't calling anybody stupid. I was calling Nobody stupid," and Jonathan laughed at the way it sounded. "Get it?"

"You just called Nobody stupid," Ellen said stubbornly.

"Well, that's what I said. I said I . . . oh, never mind. Come on."

"I *am* coming on."

They pulled their tractors and Jonathan pretended he was driving a race car on a speedway and that he had on a helmet and goggles and everything.

As they settled into an even pace toward the bus stop, Jonathan kept checking his tractor. He wasn't watching Nobody. Then he heard the loud, uneven sound of Mr. Dennihan's truck. Quickly, Jonathan tried to grab Nobody. He was too late and Nobody darted toward the fast-moving truck, which rattled and seemed only loosely connected, barely holding together.

"Nobody! Come back here," Jonathan shouted.

It didn't do any good and Nobody was prepared to bark at the wheels of the truck when suddenly be began to scramble backwards, trying desperately to get out of the way of the truck.

Dennihan's truck bore down on them. Jonathan could see red-faced Dennihan grinning as if it were great sport as he swung the truck right toward them.

Grabbing Ellen roughly by the shoulder, Jonathan scampered toward the ditch off the shoulder of the road.

Just as the right front wheel hit the edge of the pavement, only inches from Nobody, Dennihan whipped the truck back away from them and never slowed down.

Ellen screamed after the truck, "Don't you do that! Don't you. . . ."

The truck was gone and Jonathan was breathing hard. Nobody actually looked startled. Jonathan felt anger well up in him and burning in his eyes.

"He tried to run over Nobody," Ellen said, her voice quavering. "He's so mean."

"I'd . . . I'd kill him if he hit Nobody," Jonathan said, the words sputtering out. The anger kept swelling up in him and he shook his head.

"Why would he do that?" Ellen asked, hurt and puzzlement in her voice.

"I don't know," Jonathan said. "I don't know." He shook his head again. It was such a mean thing to do, so deliberately cruel, that Jonathan could hardly believe it. Why would anyone do that, he wondered to himself, and all the while he could see Mr. Dennihan's face, red and grinning, and bearing down on them, with Nobody trying to run backwards as fast as he had been running forward.

Jonathan put his hand on Nobody's head as they walked. Nobody seemed more subdued. They rounded another short curve and could see the bus-stop down a slight incline in front of them. Ellen carried her tractor now and walked in the soft, powdery dust-like sand off the edge of the road. Jonathan glanced back at his tractor every few steps and began to wish he had left it at home.

Chapter Four

The bus-stop—the end of the line—was at a crossroads. The intersecting road was not much wider than a driveway. A brook ran parallel to the road. Just as Jonathan and Ellen approached the stop, the small, rickety, top-heavy bus lurched into view. They quickened their steps and got there just as the bus sighed to a stop. Jonathan smelled the oily exhaust and felt the heat that surrounded the tiny bus as if it was something alive.

The driver smiled down at them as he spoke to their mother, who stood waiting for the door to open. The door opened with a hesitant shudder and their mother stepped out as lightly as making a grand entrance from the most elegant form of transpor-tation in the entire world.

Irene Clayton's smile radiated at Jonathan and Ellen so that Jonathan knew they were the most important and dearest things possible for her. She held out her arms. "My little blond-headed rag-a-muffins."

Then their mother asked, as she did every afternoon, "How did your day go?" Just as regularly, they would answer, "Fine." That was part of the ritual, and once these formalities were over, they got on with the business of relating events of the day and other thoughts that mattered. In a way, Jonathan liked the routine because it gave a framework or a set of rules of manners that they lived by. So many things in Jonathan's life seemed uprooted, especially since the business failed and they had to come here to live, that anything that helped make things seem more normal gave him comfort.

But today, before they got into the exchange, Ellen blurted out, "Mr. Dennihan tried to run over Nobody."

They stepped away from the bus, which shuddered, then backed into the intersecting road, swung around and coughed and wheezed away.

"What?" Her voice pitched high. Irene's face showed every emotion clearly and Jonathan knew the effect the news would have. Any hint of cruelty to animals or children caused deep instant anger in her.

"That's right," Ellen said, nodding her head for emphasis, a mannerism she had picked up at school that spring from her teacher. Ellen was all the time picking up the ways other people did things, Jonathan knew.

Irene studied each of them as they walked toward Aunt Eva's. "Tell me," she said.

In telling, Jonathan embellished only a bit. Ellen interrupted once or twice with a few details of her own.

"Maybe he didn't mean to," Irene said when Jonathan finished.

Jonathan knew his mother did not really believe that Dennihan had done it by mistake. But she said what she said the same way their father would have, Jonathan knew, for possible comfort, not for truth.

"He meant it all right," Ellen said, pouting her lower lip in a determined way. Jonathan recognized that mannerism as one of her very own.

"We could see him looking and kind of laughing," Jonathan said.

"He's mean," Ellen said, holding to her mother's free hand.

Irene did not say anything but stared straight ahead and Jonathan could tell she was thinking about it. Looking at his mother, he knew she was pretty but usually never thought about it until someone made a remark about it, and then he would see her anew, her dark curly hair, like David's, and green eyes and would realize it all over again. Even when people did not say she was pretty, he could tell by the way they stared at her—the men smiling and shifting their weight and holding their shoulders up and the women with rather tight lips, staring at her—that they thought she was pretty. All the while their mother chattered away or went happily about her business and seemed not to notice.

Still prancing about, full of himself, Nobody kept thumping his heavy tail against Jonathan's legs and almost knocking Jonathan off balance as he walked.

Ellen pointed to the small paper shopping bag Irene carried. "What's that?"

"Oh, just some lace for the dolls," Irene said, "and two little candy bars we'll eat upstairs after supper."

Lace for dolls and candy for children. Jonathan knew nothing in the world represented his mother's wish for the world anymore than that.

Then Jonathan decided, after all, that Nobody was all right and he wanted her cheerful again so he told her about the dam. He was very enthusiastic about the swimming hole and Ellen joined in the telling.

"How deep is it?" Irene asked.

"Oh, it's not deep at all. Barely deep enough to swim in."

"It's not dangerous," Ellen said, adding solemnly, with her head bobbing to give her words extra weight: "And none of us will ever go down there alone. We use the button system."

"The buddy system," Jonathan corrected. "Where you buddy looks after you. Not a button system. Whoever heard of such a thing?"

"That's good. I don't want any of you to go down there alone. All go together or no one goes."

"While we were there," Ellen said, "ol' Hubert Dennihan was spying on us."

"What do you mean spying?"

"While we were building the dam," Jonathan said. "He was hiding in the bushes across the creek watching us."

"Maybe he just wanted to play with you."

"We weren't playing," Jonathan said. "We were building a dam. And he kept on hanging around. I think. At least David saw him just when we finished."

"He was probably just lonesome and wanted to play, or help you build the dam."

Jonathan pushed aside a twinge of pity for Hubert by saying, "We don't like him. He's just, well, he just isn't much."

"I know you don't. I can probably understand why, but I do feel sorry for him, with that father and only his mother. . . ."

Ellen spoke up authoritatively, "But, Mother, just feeling sorry for him doesn't mean you like him and want to play with him."

And that ended that. Irene could not hide a slight smile. Jonathan was determined to take Ellen's approach: There was absolutely no sense in feeling bad because you did not want to have anything to do with red-headed old Hubert Dennihan.

They rounded the last, long curve and could see the cemetery up ahead. Irene looked at it and away. Jonathan took quick glances over his shoulder at his tractor and saw the lengthening, gangly shadow he made.

Irene asked if there had been any mail and they said no. "I was hoping we'd hear from your daddy today." She stared ahead at the road and then quickly smiled and said, "Well, what will we read tonight? The last chapter, isn't it, of *The Secret Garden*?" Almost every night, while they were piled around on the big bed, she read to all of them, including Cortland and Till.

A moment later Ellen asked, "When can we go live with him?"

She still held to her mother's hand and carried her tractor in her other hand.

Jonathan spoke up before his mother could answer, repeating those phrases, almost by rote, he had heard so often, "He's got to get settled in a job and get finances sort of straightened out first." His mother had uttered those words, his aunt and uncle had, and he had heard his father repeating them until, while they stood for an explanation of life as they were then living it, the words, weighed by themselves, meant little to Jonathan. He knew, hauntingly, that there was so much more to it than that. Those were phrases they canted, the same as they said they were fine when asked how they were doing. They served as a blanket for whatever truth lay underneath. Jonathan knew that their family loved the truth but kept it often unspoken and clutched to the breast in fear that it might hurt someone, and instead often communicated with words of encouragement and optimism that fooled no one, but words that everyone accepted; they were words spoken with love.

Perhaps Irene sensed that the message the words were supposed to carry might be lost. So she added, "Yes. Your father will take us with him. We'll go with him when things are a more settled."

"But he's got to find a job first," Jonathan said. "I wish he already had one or I wish he hadn't gone out of business." Then with a burst of feeling he said, "Or I wish he was a judge or a lawyer or something like Uncle Roy or somebody and didn't have to be out trying to find a job." Jonathan knew his wishes were not so much for his father as for something to ease the vague, less-than-worthy feeling it gave him for his father not to have a job. That spring at the country school he had lied to the other boys and said his father had a job in Washington, and that they were just staying here temporarily because his father was working so hard in Washington. He doubted if the other students believed him and he was ashamed for himself and for his father.

"Well, your father is not a judge or a lawyer," Irene said firmly. "And as a matter of fact Uncle Roy is no longer a judge. That was years ago. And your father is really a school teacher more than anything else and then your grandfather was going to put him in business, and that's when you grandfather got sick and there wasn't any money to back the business . . . and . . . and your father may not be the best businessman in the world but he's your father and he's trying real hard, I'm sure."

Jonathan felt awful.

His mother put her arm around his shoulders and pulled him to her as they walked. She momentarily freed her hand from Ellen's and brushed back the hair from Jonathan's eyes. She smiled the bright, child-like, full-of-enthusiasm smile. "Meanwhile, isn't this a lovely place to spend the summer? The mountains, the pretty trees, and flowers . . . and now your own private swimming pool."

"I thought you said the mountains made you sad," Ellen said.

"My poor, melancholy babies. No, the mountains don't always make me sad. Just sometimes. That day I told your daddy that, well, that was just a day that I was sad."

Jonathan remembered it well. The day in early March they drove toward Asheville, the old Plymouth, which was sold shortly after they arrived, packed almost to overflowing with personal belongings, his mother and father, the three children and Nobody. They had seen the range of mountains late in the afternoon sun, growing larger and changing from purple to a deep greenish-blue and then purple again as it got later in the afternoon. Joel Clayton pointed them out happily; he had been born among them. Irene had originally been from the Coastal Plains of the state.

"They're stately, dignified," his father had said.

"They're gloomy," Irene answered.

Jonathan's father smiled at her and to himself. "Oh, Irene, they're not gloomy. It's just your mood."

She sat there, hands folded in her lap. Ellen was squeezed in between them with her blond head on her mother's shoulder. Irene said quietly, "No, it's not my mood. They make me sad."

Joel took the cigar from his mouth and held it gently between two fingers. He glanced at her and back to the road in front of him. "I'm sorry they do," he said softly. "I'm sorry they do."

Jonathan immediately decided mountains made

him sad too.

David spoke up loudly, "I love 'em." He leaned back manfully in the rear seat and repeated a phrase he heard on one of the many radio programs he listened to. "They're full of mystery, intrigue and great adventure."

Then Irene said something that sounded so strange coming from her. "They're filed with dying." She must have realized how it sounded, so she smiled brightly. "Oh, I was just teasing. Mountains can be pretty." She patted Ellen's leg and looked down at her, then back at the horizon, a little smile pulling at her eyes. "They *are* rather overwhelming, just the same."

And now, walking along Mattaskeet Road, Ellen said, "Mother, why do Uncle Roy and Aunt Eva talk about Daddy?"

"What do you mean?"

"You know. They talk about him working, or not working, and being in Washington and all."

Jonathan saw the flicker of pain that played across his mother's face. Jonathan had heard the talk himself.

Irene said, "They were just discussing the bad luck your father has had in business and with finances."

"I don't like it when they talk about him," Ellen said.

"They don't mean any harm. After all, Aunt Eva is your daddy's sister."

Ellen was quiet a moment. "Is she your aunt, too?"

"Oh, Ellen," she said with a smile, "I've explained it to you before. She's my sister-in-law. She's your daddy's sister and my sister-in-law because I'm married to her brother."

"What about Uncle Roy? Then is he your uncle-in-law?"

Jonathan said, "Aw, Ellen, don't be so dumb."

"Don't call each other dumb," Irene said. She turned her face to the sky as they started up the long rocky driveway. Her expression was one of calmness as she looked at the sky. "Isn't the sky beautiful?"

The last rays of the sun touched the tips of the mountains and the clouds so that the sky had become a great glob of red and gold and orange, and it all looked to Jonathan as though the colors had been stirred together with a giant wooden cooking spoon. Maybe it was because of the sky and its colors and because he was walking quietly beside his mother, but he suddenly felt an overflowing of happiness, an almost unspeakable joy and a sense that everything was all right in the world, and that this feeling would go on and on, and that somehow, in some way, he would do great and wonderful things in the world, and that his mother and father and all of them would be happy forever.

It must have been at just about that moment, Jonathan realized later, that Mr. Dennihan drunkenly took a swing with his fist at his wife as she cowered on the tiny front porch of their pigpen house; he missed, lost his balance, staggered and fell face forward down the steps, breaking his left arm at the elbow.

Chapter Five

They were seated at the big, heavy wooden table in the kitchen, preparing to have supper, when they heard Hubert Dennihan.

Hubert stood by the kitchen window calling Uncle Roy. "Mr. Britton! Mr. Britton!" His voice had the thin mountaineer twang to it so that he stretched out the first syllable of the name twice as long as most people would say it.

Uncle Roy cocked his head to one side.

"It's ol' Hubert," Till said.

Pushing her chair back and getting up, Aunt Eva said, "I wonder what in the world he wants?" Uncle Roy slowly folded his napkin but did not get up right away. Aunt Eva started toward the back porch. She was puzzled, as she said, as they all were, for while Mr. Dennihan frequently came to pick up the garbage, do odd jobs and borrow and repay money, neither Hubert nor Mrs. Dennihan had ever come here to the house. Jonathan had seen Hubert in the pasture, on the road and infrequently at

school that spring. But he had never seen him at his
uncle's house.

David and Till got up and followed Aunt Eva to
the back porch. Cortland kept eating. Jonathan got
up, too, and his mother said, "No, children . . . oh,
well. . . ."

Hubert stood by the back steps, his red hair
wild, and his eyes showed he had been crying. He
wore only a pair of short pants and his thin legs had
water spatters on them through the dust and dirt. He
spoke quickly, sing-song, gulping in his breath.
"Mrs. Britton. Daddy's hurt himself. His arm is
broke, he thinks."

Aunt Eva turned toward the kitchen. "Roy," she
called, then turned back to Hubert. "What in the
world happened? How did he . . . broken, not broke
. . . Roy!"

"I'm coming." Uncle Roy moved solemnly
toward them. Jonathan and the others made room
for him. "What's the matter?"

"Daddy wants you to take him to the doctor if
you can. He can't drive. That's why I come over. He
fell off the porch. Down the steps. And his arm—
this arm—is broke, he thinks."

"How'd he fall off the porch?" David asked.

"Him and Mother was, was fussing. . . ." His
voice trailed. Hubert glanced about him at the
people standing there and Jonathan thought a trace
of embarrassment flickered across his face, as if he
were not sure, but suspected that some people did
not fight with each other as his father did with his
mother.

Uncle Roy asked, "Is your mother all right?" His voice sounded soft and kind but judicial and Jonathan could picture him as a judge.

"Yeah, yes sir," Hubert looked first at Uncle Roy and at the people staring at him and then at the ground. "He missed her when he hit at her. That's when he fell. Down the steps."

"I see," Uncle Roy said, and then to Eva, "Keep a plate of supper for me. I'll check this out. Take him to the doctor. Call Dr. Proctor and tell him I'm on my way. Meet him at his office." Uncle Roy touched Aunt Eva's arm, a sort of pat and the closest Jonathan saw them passing little signs of affection.

As Uncle Roy strode toward his car, a black Nash sedan, Hubert began to run toward his pigpen-house. Uncle Roy called him and told him to get in the front seat with him. Hubert grinned and climbed up into the car like a monkey. He sat with his back straight, head high, in the front passenger's seat, the big grin still on his face.

Jonathan felt as though he almost liked Hubert then, or at least felt a sadness for him, which was not too far from fondness, Jonathan figured.

Till said, "Look at him sitting up there with that smirk on his face. He really thinks he's something."

Cortland had come out for the tail-end of the conversation. He chewed a mouthful of food. "Bet his daddy's arm's not broken anyway. Just fractured."

"Come on back in for supper," Aunt Eva said. The car, driven old-man stiffly, as always, headed around the driveway out of sight.

Back in the kitchen, supper resumed. The evening meal always consisted of two or three vegetables, some cooked for hours, a main meat dish of something like country-fried steak or pork chops or chicken. Always there was a large blue and white pitcher of milk and the homemade butter that Aunt Eva turned out with a small hand-paddle churn. Sometimes there might be a dish of country ham slices and occasionally Aunt Eva fried a taste or two of what they called streak-of-lean, a salted piece of pork belly that had not been cured into bacon. Jonathan liked to chew on the meat skin from the streak-of-lean, and he would chew it until it turned white and became frayed and then he swallowed the little pieces.

Each had his own napkin and napkin ring. Jonathan frequently managed to pick up the wrong one and could never understand his aunt's well-controlled horror that perhaps someone might be using the wrong napkin.

Grace, or as they called it, the blessing, was intoned by Uncle Roy, which he had done this evening when they first sat down. After the blessing, mild chaos always reigned for a few minutes while dishes crisscrossed, despite Aunt Eva's efforts to have them proceed orderly in one direction. Jonathan knew that his mother was often guilty of starting some of the dishes in a counter fashion and he suspected she did this just to keep things lively. His mother always fixed herself a small individual salad, no matter what kind of salad Aunt Eva prepared.

"What's fractured?" Jonathan asked.

"Same as broken, almost. Maybe not quite as bad," David said.

"Is broken when his arm comes all the way off?" Ellen asked.

"Aw, don't be so dumb, Ellen," Jonathan said.

"Don't call each other dumb," Irene said. She was busy putting vinegar and sugar on her sliced tomatoes. Aunt Eva saw her and frowned slightly.

"No, dear," Aunt Eva explained, still watching Irene but talking to Ellen. "If the arm is taken off, that's an amputation. If it's broken or fractured the bone inside is just cracked. Usually you can't even tell from looking at it."

"Little Richard's leg was probably fractured that time," their mother said, daintily adding salt and pepper to the tomatoes. "But it got all right. Remember?" She spoke of a pet rabbit they had in Georgia.

"Oh, yes," Ellen said.

They settled down again to eat. No one said anything about the tomatoes except Cortland and Aunt Eva told him there was nothing wrong with them, that they were just fixed differently. Once during the meal David and Till got to whispering and giggling about something. Aunt Eva told them they should behave properly at the table. Irene just smiled in their general direction.

For dessert, Aunt Eva served blackberry cobbler with thick cream. The cobbler had a chewy crust where a lot of the sweetness seemed to seep.

Jonathan liked this part the best. When they finished, Aunt Eva smoked a cigarette through her yellowed ivory holder. Irene began humming softly. Aunt Eva tried to smile a bit and blew a thin trail of cigarette smoke toward the ceiling.

Irene spoke: "I've got a little boy who is so fascinated with your cigarettes I'm afraid he'll start smoking when he's older."

Jonathan did not know she was watching. And yet it was so much like her, he knew. He would think she was a billion miles away until suddenly she would say something and he knew she was very much aware of everything around her.

All talk about the Dennihans with Jonathan and the others had been curbed by Aunt Eva. The topic had just been hushed up again when Irene spoke out, "Something bad is going to happen over there." She drummed lightly, rhythmically on her tea glass with her fingernails. She could make a dramatic statement like that and have Jonathan completely mesmerized, eyes wide, waiting for the next chapter.

"What do you mean?" Aunt Eva asked.

"Something bad will happen."

"Oh, I don't know. I don't like to think so anyway." Then dropping her somewhat reserved pose, Aunt Eva gave way to curiosity and turned toward Irene, who still hummed lightly and tapped on the glass. "What makes you say that, Irene?"

"He's drinking more, for one thing."

"I *have* noticed that this summer . . . well, yes, he does seem to be." Then, "Children, do you want to go on outside and play a while?"

Cortland said yes but the others were slow moving away from the table. Jonathan wanted to listen.

Aunt Eva said, "But maybe this, this accident will serve to wake him up a bit."

"No. It'll probably make him worse," Irene said. "He'll feel sorry for himself and he won't be able to work as much and when a man hasn't got his work, any kind of work, then . . . it's not very good." Jonathan could tell that toward the end of what she said she thought about his father. Jonathan sat very still.

"Come on, children," Aunt Eva said, looking at Jonathan and the way he leaned forward, arms on the table, and stared at his mother, "why not go outside and play?" They began to shuffle their chairs around, preparing to go but with a certain delay.

Irene stood up, picked up her partly empty plate to carry to the sink, then smiled brightly at Aunt Eva, as if to soften what she was about to say. "If there's love over there, though, maybe nothing too bad will happen. If there's love there it'll help a lot."

As if taking up a long-standing secret argument, Aunt Eva said, "Oh, I don't think there has to be real, *real* love like you read about."

"Yes, there does," Irene said quietly, rinsing off her plate.

Jonathan and the others went outside. He knew somehow that his mother, standing there by the sink and speaking so softly, had been summing up that which she firmly believed, held on to.

Chapter Six

It was dusk and the mountain air was cooling and felt good. The five of them went around to the sloping front yard with its evergreen bushes, the huge cluster of rose of Sharon, the cedar hedge and trees—oak, a poplar and two dogwoods. As they had been doing the past several nights, they played the razzle-dazzle game of tag of their evenings they called Ain't No Big Bears Out Tonight. With David counting the eeni-meenie, Ellen ended up being the first "it," as usual.

They darted away from her while she counted, but Jonathan could not get caught up in the spirit of the game and ran over to one edge of the yard and stopped to look over across the meadow and Mattaskeet Creek to Clown Mountain.

"You're it," Ellen squealed, tagging him on the arm.

He got back into the game and only glanced once more at Clown Mountain. There must have been more wind at the top of the mountain, for the clown swayed, laughing, Jonathan was sure, over some secret.

After the tag that night and after the baths, they settled on the two double-beds in the large room upstairs that Irene used and listened to her read. It was not the last chapter of *The Secret Garden*, after all, but one that did a lot of explaining. Irene sat rather primly and still in the rocking chair, holding the book. They were all in their pajamas, including Cortland and Till, who also listened to her read each night. Ellen and Jonathan were on one bed and David, Cortland and Till sprawled on the other. Several times Irene had to speak to David and Till because they giggled and squirmed. Ellen slept in this room with her mother; David and Jonathan slept in a smaller room that had been used for storage; Till and Cortland each had their own tiny bedrooms on each side of the bathroom.

Jonathan did not like the room his mother had. It was not just because with its stuffy, guest-room appearance (despite the clutter at one corner where she did her doll sewing) it did not resemble her at all, but partly because of a picture on the wall by the closet. The old-fashion looking photograph was of an unsmiling infant who had died when less than a year old. The picture bothered Jonathan. He always thought of it as having been taken after death. The picture was tinted and that gave it a curiously ominous appearance because the colors looked unreal. The eyes were pale blue and the hair an unnatural looking light brown. The gown the infant wore, with its lace-trimmed neck, seemed faded yellow and antique. When he first noticed the picture, Jonathan had asked his mother who the baby was. She had stared at it, then turned away, saying, "Someone dear to Aunt Eva."

One afternoon, shortly after they had come there to stay, Jonathan had run upstairs for something and found Aunt Eva standing before the portrait. The way her shoulders sagged made her look smaller. Her face was very still. Jonathan had been puzzled at first about Aunt Eva coming upstairs at all, something she rarely did. She turned toward Jonathan, took off her glasses, secured with a black ribbon, and let them fall gently to her breast. She whispered, "Oh, you children . . . you wonderful children." She embraced Jonathan. He stood there stiffly and could feel the glasses between them, and he sensed it was not really him that she hugged so closely to her.

Later Jonathan learned that the child had been Aunt Eva's by her first marriage. Barely seventeen, she had married a young man from Virginia, who everyone said could charm the stripes off a snake, but was too wild to be tie d down. She had moved away with him to Charlottesville where the child, a boy, was born, there to die of scarlet fever when ten months old. That same month, the young husband, singing and roaring drunk, had driven one of his buggies he kept for sport as fast as the horse would run. A wheel on the buggy collapsed in a deep rut and he had been thrown out, striking his head on rocks beside the road. He lived until the next afternoon. Then the childless young widow, who had suffered two deaths so close together, came back home to the mountains of North Carolina. She entered the nearby teachers' college and settled to teaching in a rather cloistered private school and, in time, married Roy Britton, a lawyer close to twelve years her senior. She was thirty when Till was born.

But Jonathan never learned why the photograph was virtually hidden away upstairs. Roy Britton certainly did not strike anyone as the type who would be jealous of a dead man's dead child. Jonathan thought that it must have been the pain that he saw in Aunt Eva's eyes when he walked in the room that made her want to keep the picture here, and he tried not to look at it when he was in the room.

Irene had been reading for several minutes when they heard Uncle Roy's car straining up the driveway; the gears shifted long past when they should have been, so that the car shuddered and sounded as if it were going to stall before he put it in a lower gear. David jumped from the bed and peered out the window. Irene told them to be still and quiet and she would go downstairs to find out what the doctor had said. Uncle Roy and Eva's bedroom was downstairs, just off the living room.

They remained quiet until Irene got part of the way downstairs, then began the usual scuffling, pinching and poking. They almost choked trying to keep from laughing out loud. Once Ellen started to cry but was laughing again by the time they heard Irene call something back to Aunt Eva and Uncle Roy as she started up the stairs.

She looked at them, sitting solemn but red-faced when she came into the room. She did not say anything to them, just sat in her chair and picked up the book from the cluttered little table beside it.

"What'd the doctor say?" David asked.

"His arm is broken, or fractured. Not too bad but he has to keep it in a cast for a few weeks."

"Was he sorry about trying to hit her?" Ellen asked.

"I don't know." She began to read and they were quiet, listening to her voice and the words flowing. Once Jonathan heard Nobody bark and some other distant noises of the night. Jonathan was almost asleep when she finished reading and they went quietly to their rooms. She kissed them goodnight and Jonathan stretched out in the cool bed as far as he could.

David talked softly about the swimming hole and the dam and about plans for tomorrow. His voice sounded husky, lying on his back with his chin on his chest. Jonathan just listened but did not answer.

Then, just as he was going to sleep he heard his mother talking downstairs with Uncle Roy and Aunt Eva. He could not understand all of the words but he heard his mother say something about how she was sure that he was trying the best he could. Jonathan knew that she was defending his father, and Jonathan missed him and wished that he was there with them and most of all he wished his father had a job and took command and was in charge of things.

Chapter Seven

The next morning at the breakfast table, Cortland said, "There are two big ones and three little ones." He tried to keep the mouthful of oatmeal from spewing out as he talked.

Jonathan watched the way Cortland poked at the food in the corners of his mouth. Aunt Eva saw Cortland doing that and got after him, saying not to talk with his mouth full.

Cortland spoke of the metal washtubs in the garage by the washing machine. They had already asked permission to take them down to the swimming hole, agreeing among themselves to ask about the washtubs before they sat down very orderly and well-behaved to eat breakfast in the kitchen with Aunt Eva. Uncle Roy and Jonathan's mother had already gone into town to work.

Jonathan stared at the cantaloupe he was eating and thought about Cortland. Even if Cortland was sort of sloppy and was forever eating or talking about eating, Jonathan marveled at how Cortland could remember numbers of things. Cortland always saw things as numbers; Jonathan saw the tubs as just a bunch of tubs, no specific number or sizes. Cortland knew exactly how many there were, big ones and small ones. It was the same when it came to dividing candy or anything else. Cortland had it all figured out. Jonathan vowed to himself, without whipping up a whole lot of enthusiasm for it, to start counting things carefully, to start paying attention to numbers.

Everyone but Till already had on what passed for bathing suits. Till went upstairs to change. Ellen, who had a navy blue wool-like, itchy-looking bathing suit with a tiny hole on one hip, had decided today to wear shorts and a little sleeveless polo shirt. The boys just wore short pants.

They went into the room off from the garage that served as the laundry room and gathered up the galvanized washtubs. Struggling and stumbling, they took the washtubs down across the road and the meadow to the creek. Nobody, not pretending to stay in the fenced area, trotted along beside Jonathan.

As they crossed the meadow, Jonathan looked up at the Dennihan's house. He didn't see anyone. Dennihan's truck was parked beside the house. Jonathan thought about the truck and reached down and patted Nobody's head.

The swimming hole looked larger to Jonathan than it had the afternoon before.

"It's past that mark," David said, pointing to one of the large roots of the maple. He sounded to

Jonathan again as if he were trying to act on radio.

They got into the water, which made them shiver at first so that Jonathan stood in the water half-crouching, his knees together and elbows by his sides. But after they got used to it they splashed around and then brought the washtubs in and tried to get in them to use as individual boats. Climbing into them face-first, the tubs tipped too far toward them and sank. They managed to get dunked many, many times before they mastered the art of backing up to the tubs, holding the tubs in place behind them, then jumping up and landing bottom-first in the tubs, arms and legs dangling out for balance. Then they were able to paddle them like tug boats. They laughed and knocked the water at each other and bumped into each other. David organized sides and strategies for naval battles.

Twice Jonathan managed to sink Cortland by sneaking his foot under Cortland's tub and giving it a sharp push that started sloshing water into it. It took very little extra water before the tubs would list and sink. Cortland caught Jonathan at it and told the others and Jonathan had to stop it.

By late morning they crawled onto the bank and lay stretched out in the sun. Jonathan watched his chest as it rose and fell with his breathing. He rolled over on his stomach in the prickly grass and could feel his heart beating.

They lay there quietly for a while when Till whispered, "There's ol' Hubert again."

Cortland stood up and tried to look menacing. He clinched his fists. "I'm going to tell him to get away."

Then David surprised Jonathan by saying, "Oh, leave him alone. He's not hurting anything. Just watching."

It surprised Jonathan for David to say that because he had thought of David as being with Till and Cortland in wanting Hubert away. Partly, too, Jonathan thought of David as having no feeling about it one way or the other. He always saw David as practical, realistic, able to build and do things, run fast and, above all, with amazing skill, hide any emotion or feeling, if he had any emotion or feeling outside of that which he learned on the radio, a fact Jonathan sometimes doubted.

Hubert, in what seemed his perpetual pose, half-crouched in the bushes across the creek from them.

More curious than hopeful, Jonathan asked, "Do you want to tell him he can play with us?"

Till snapped her head toward Jonathan. "No! Absolutely not."

David watched him silently.

"What are you doing there?" Till yelled.

"I can stand here if I want to," Hubert said, straightening up from his crouch. "You don't own the whole world."

"This is our swimming pool, though," Till said.

"We made it," Cortland said.

"So what? I don't want your ol' swimming hole anyway."

"What are you always spying at us for?" Cortland said, looking to Till and David for support.

"I'm not," Hubert said. Then drew himself up

as much as he could, glanced over his shoulder—
Lord knows why—and back at them and said with a
strained bass to his voice, "To *hell* with your
swimming hole!" Then he paused to see how hell
would strike them, and fled.

Jonathan and the others were properly aghast.
They had been taught, and believed firmly, that it
was extremely wicked to use even the mildest swear
words unless you were well over twenty-one and
then only in real emergencies such as when you hit
your finger with a hammer or got honked at by
another motorist just because you were drifting to
his side of the road while trying to light your cigar,
as was the case with Jonathan's father from time to
time. Once Jonathan had said damn when he was
walking alone back to Aunt Eva's house from
playing with his soldiers. He just wanted to see what
it sounded like. He said it out loud, "Damn!" It
sounded awful and he immediately was embarrassed
and ashamed. The word sounded a little puny, too,
when he said it. He promised he was not going to
say it at all again until he was at least twenty-one and
maybe not at all then.

Till's eyes were wide. "Did you hear what he
said?"

They watched Hubert disappear.

Later they turned back to the water and their
still-private swimming hole. While David, Till and
Cortland played again with their washtubs, Ellen and
Jonathan waded up into the shallow end of the
swimming hole where the water ran clear and cold
on their ankles. They looked at pebbles and crawfish

or whatever else they could find. They were poking around, feeling the water run over their hands and wrists when over to his right Jonathan saw the crescent-shaped white rock that almost sparkled as the water ran over it. The rock was smaller than his fists held together. In the water the thin edge and point looked sharper than they were. Except for one drop of brownish coloration, it was pure white. Jonathan picked it up. "Wow, look at this," he called. Ellen drew near and they waded back to the others.

"Eureka," Till said. "He's found a diamond or something."

The way she said it made Jonathan a little mad. "Well, it *is* pretty," he said.

Till and David and Cortland had stopped with the tubs and had been practicing swimming under water with their eyes open. Till's eyes looked wet and her eyelashes stuck together in points. Her dark hair was plastered down, almost touching her shoulders.

"Hey," David said, "that's just what we need to dive for. That can be our lost treasure or something. And we can see it easy underwater."

Laughing, Jonathan tossed the rock into the deepest part of the water. It landed near Till and she came up with it clutched in her hand high above her head, her eyes wet and wide open. "Eureka!" she shouted.

That was the name they gave the rock and that noon when they trudged back to the house carrying their washtubs, Jonathan also carried Eureka. It became one of his duties to keep up with it and he carried it with him every time after that they went down to the creek. He kept the rock either on the back porch or up in the room on his dresser.

They played in their swimming hole at least once a day for the next few days and Jonathan carried Eureka with him until it seemed as much a part of him when they headed toward the meadow as having Nobody trot alongside him. Nobody had stopped making a pretense of staying in the fenced area.

They didn't see Hubert but once during this time and that was when he rode in the front seat of the pick-up truck with Mr. Dennihan as the two of them came down the rutted dirt road from their house toward Mattaskeet Road. Jonathan could see the sling around Dennihan's neck. The truck veered slightly when he shifted gears and tried to steer at the same time by pressing his cast against the wheel. Jonathan kept his hand on Nobody's neck. He watched and saw that Hubert and Dennihan had not looked at them.

Watching the rattle-trap black truck as it passed in line with Clown Mountain and the tree at the top, swaying in the wind as always, made Jonathan shiver. It was as if Dennihan and the truck cast a chilling shadow across them for a flicker of a moment. But then they were gone and Jonathan tried not to think about them.

Chapter Eight

It had been well over a week, almost two, since Irene had heard from their father.

Then one afternoon when they had come back to the house tired from swimming, and they had eaten supper and were downstairs in the library listening to the radio. Uncle Roy was reading his paper and muttering about Roosevelt, which Jonathan thought was almost the same thing as blasphemy. Except for Uncle Roy, he had never heard anyone criticize President Roosevelt.

The phone rang, and as Aunt Eva went into the dining room to answer it, she said as she usually did, "Now, I wonder who that could be?" She came back into the room beaming and excited. "It's Joel. On the phone from Washington. Long distance."

Uncle Roy lowered his paper. With a faint smile he said, "If he's calling from Washington I suppose it *is* long distance."

"Well, he's on the telephone anyway," Aunt Eva said.

"Wonderful," Irene said, putting down the doll's bonnet she was sewing and hurried to the dining room.

"Can we talk too?"

"We'll see," she said to Ellen. "But you children be quiet now so I can hear. It's long distance."

Till and Cortland had to stay in the library but Jonathan, David, and Ellen went with Irene into the dining room. They stood fidgeting while she spoke on the phone.

"Hello, Joel . . . Yes, we're fine . . . I've worried because we didn't hear from you. Why didn't you write? Well, I'm glad you called . . . No, I'm not cross. You just sound so, so happy, and I've been worried sick."

There was some more talk on the other end of the line, and then Irene's face began to grow into a smile and she smiled at the children. "Oh, that's wonderful. When will you know for sure? Monday? Well, this is Thursday. I *do* hope you get it. That would be, that would be so wonderful. Will you come down here as soon as you hear? Wait a minute children. They're dying to speak to you. I'll let them and then I want to talk to you again."

He spoke to each one of them in turn and called them pet names and said he loved them. Ellen asked him when they could come live with him. Jonathan, when he heard his father's voice and he seemed so much closer, felt bad about being ashamed of his father's not having a job. And when Jonathan's father said he loved him, Jonathan said he loved him too but he felt guilty about the way he had been thinking about his father and wishing his father was different.

When Irene talked again to him, she said she would be waiting for his call Monday night and that she would keep her fingers crossed. She said she would say a prayer and that sounded strange to Jonathan. The only time she talked about prayers was to occasionally tell Jonathan and the others to say their prayers before going to bed. They had all learned the Lord's Prayer and they could say it quickly. Once in a while she said the Lord's Prayer with them and she made them slow down.

Then they all went happily and noisily back into the library. Irene spoke excitedly to Uncle Roy and Aunt Eva. "He's been interviewed for a job that looks like he may get. He's almost positive. He's got to go back on Monday for a final answer and he'll let us know for sure then."

"What is the job?" Uncle Roy asked.

"It's with a publishing company. Sales work to schools and libraries, I think he said. Books. Either textbooks or encyclopedias. That's about all I know. Oh, I just have a feeling he'll get it." She went on breathlessly. "If he does—if the answer is yes on Monday—he's coming down here for two weeks before he starts to work and we'll go back with him . . . and get settled. But he's not really sure where it would be. He thinks Washington."

"I don't want to sound like a wet blanket," Aunt Eva said, "but I know how overly optimistic Joel can get, and you do too, Irene, and I just hope he's not counting his eggs . . . his chickens . . . that he's not being overly optimistic."

"I feel sure he'll get it," Irene said, still somewhat breathless.

They were all in good spirits that night when they went to bed. Jonathan felt good the next day and felt bigger inside. Twice he spoke back to Till when she tried to say something smart to him. David took time to try to explain to Ellen what the District of Columbia is and how when their father was calling he was in Washington, which is in the District of Columbia and it isn't quite like a state. He was very patient and acted much older, Jonathan thought. And Ellen sat there and starred at David as he talked and squinted her eyes and tried to understand what he was talking about but Jonathan could tell by looking at her she didn't know diddly-squat about what David was saying. He was wasting his time.

Jonathan realized, for the first time, that here was something—their sister Ellen—that Jonathan knew more about than David. To Jonathan, it was one of the first glimmerings that perhaps he was not totally inferior to his older brother. He knew it was sort of silly, but it was something. He knew Ellen better than David did.

The good feeling, the optimism, seemed to buoy everyone the next day or so, even though the talking about it was kept down somewhat as if the talking might jinx the whole thing. But by Monday night at nine, when their father had not called, it began to show on their mother, and the rest of them. Irene sat rather strained and quiet. Jonathan kept on watching her without saying anything. When she started helping them get ready for bed, she acted like she forgot what she was doing once or twice and had to do things over.

At almost eleven the phone rang and Jonathan and David waked up with a start. Even though the phone was downstairs, they could hear the loud ring. Their mother and Aunt Eva and Uncle Roy were still up, Jonathan realized. Faintly, he heard his mother on the phone. After the telephone conversation, their mother talked with Aunt Eva and Uncle Roy a little longer. She sounded tired. Jonathan heard her say, in answer to a question from Aunt Eva, "Maybe drinking just a little bit but not very much."

Then she came back upstairs and sat on the edge of the bed. Jonathan and David went into the room; Ellen stirred and rubbed her eyes. Their father still did not know for sure, she told them. He would try to let them know something tomorrow night Jonathan went to bed thinking why in the world his father couldn't just go ahead and get the job and not worry his mother half to death and keep everybody upset and make Jonathan feel ashamed of him, all over again.

The next morning their mother carried with her to work two small dolls she had dressed. She would try to sell them at the shop. She still seemed tired and talked very little. Jonathan felt awful. That afternoon she called and said she was too hot and tired to ride the bus so she was going to wait for Uncle Roy and ride home with him. It seemed funny to Jonathan not to walk down to meet her in the evening. Ellen and Jonathan were sitting out by the big oak tree with Nobody when she and Uncle Roy drove up. She waved and smiled but did not seem really and truly happy like she usually did, Jonathan thought.

Supper was sort of quiet and afterwards they went outside and did not really get excited with playing. Their mother came walking around the side of the house later on and Ellen and Jonathan stood with her while she looked at the flowers and shrubs planted near the front porch steps. Every now and then she would pull at a little leaf or delicately touch a flower with the toe of her shoe, to move the flower's face so she could look at it.

They were upstairs getting ready for bed when the phone rang. Irene stood very still in the middle of the room listening until she heard Aunt Eva call her. Jonathan and the others stayed at the head of the stairs where their mother had told them to stay. There was a moment of soft talking and then their mother said happily, "Oh, Joel, that's wonderful . . . oh, wonderful!"

David grinned and pulled Ellen's hair and she hit him in the chest with her little fist and laughed.

When Irene came back upstairs afterwards, she sang to herself and kept interrupting her soft singing to talk again about how things were going to be from now on.

Jonathan lay in bed trying to think about how good everything would be but he couldn't imagine Washington except for the Washington Monument and he had a hard time getting his father to come real to him in his mind and heart so he thought about being close to him and smelling cigar smoke but that only helped a little.

Chapter Nine

Early the next morning they ate breakfast and laughed and then hurried down to the swimming hole.

But as they got close they knew it didn't look right. They stopped. David kept shaking his head with quick little jerks, as if he couldn't believe it. The swimming hole was gone. The pool was empty. Someone had used a long pole, which still lay across one of the burlap bags, to pry out the middle section of the dam. The pool was gone and the creek was almost back to normal.

"Hubert did it," David said. "No one else would have done it."

"Just because we wouldn't let him play in it," Cortland said.

"That's no reason," Till said.

They waded out in the shallow water and looked at the wrecked dam. Then they sat on the edge of the bank and hated Hubert and talked about what they would do to him if they caught him messing around there again. After they had sat for a long time, David talked them into getting started rebuilding the dam. He started out sounding like someone on the radio leading the attack against the Indians or something but then he began to talk more like himself as they got caught up in the spirit of it. They worked hard and by noon had it all back in place and the pool was becoming a pool again.

"I'm going to tell Mother what ol' Hubert did," Ellen said.

Jonathan, who had been quiet, ventured, cautiously, an opinion: "Maybe if we'd have let Hubert play—maybe when we weren't around—he wouldn't have done it."

Till wheeled around at Jonathan. "He had no right to do it anyway. Don't you forget that!"

"Well, I. . . ."

"What are you doing, taking up for him or something for goodness sakes?" Till demanded.

Jonathan looked at Till, then down at the ground and shook his head.

"All right, then," Till said.

David spoke up, sounding for all the world like one of the characters on the radio. "There's no justice in an evil act."

Wrinkling his nose like he didn't believe something, Cortland looked up at David and said, "Huh? What's that supposed to mean?"

David acted a little self-conscious, which was rare, Jonathan knew, grinned and said, "I think the Shadow says that."

As they trudged across the meadow going back

to the house to eat lunch, they saw Mr. Dennihan driving his truck down the rutty dirt road. He drove jerkily with that one arm in a cast. They were within a few dozen yards of him when he swung on to Mattaskeet Road and Jonathan could see Mr. Dennihan's red face and tell that he was almost drunk. Jonathan held on to Nobody's collar because he had started to bark and wanted to chase the truck.

Late that afternoon, Jonathan and Ellen walked along Mattaskeet Road to meet their mother's bus. Nobody trotted along beside them, his tongue lolling out of one side of his mouth. Jonathan and Ellen wanted to hear their mother talk about their father's coming and how happy they would all be in Washington.

They were rounding the last little curve before the short incline down to the bus-stop when they heard Mr. Dennihan's rattle-trap truck coming toward them and they glanced up. Nobody had darted a few yards toward the truck, and then stopped to watch it approach.

Jonathan called to Nobody, but the dog didn't seem ready to chase the truck anyway. He just stood there watching it approach.

Suddenly the truck swerved sharply to the left, the wheels at the edge of the road; then it careened back at a hard angle to the right, heading directly toward Nobody. The dog started to leap just as the truck was on him. But Nobody didn't have time and the right front wheel of the truck hit him and knocked him toward the high bank.

Jonathan yelled, "Nobody!"

Ellen screamed.

Dennihan jerked the truck back toward the middle of the road. Jonathan could see Dennihan's eyes open wide and his mouth open and he didn't even slow down.

Jonathan ran and knelt beside Nobody, who twitched and jerked his head up, but the rest of him stayed on the ground. Jonathan's vision was blurred because he was crying. Nobody made whimpering sounds, and tried twice to get up. His hindquarters flopped to one side and he couldn't make it. Nobody tried dragging himself with his front legs and yelped and then lay there.

Jonathan tried to touch him but Nobody yelped and acted frightened. "Oh, Nobody, be all right, be all right," Jonathan kept saying.

Ellen knelt beside Jonathan and the dog. Jonathan became aware that she squeezed his shoulder tightly. She was crying and said, "Why did he do that?"

They heard the bus pulling up to its stop and Jonathan told Ellen to run get their mother. In minutes, Irene and Ellen half ran back to Jonathan and the dog. Nobody raised his head and looked at their mother and tried to get up again but whimpered and she patted his head and tried to keep him from rolling it back and forth.

"Oh, why would he do that and not even stop?" Irene said.

"Is he going to die? Is he?" Ellen sobbed.

"Maybe he'll be all right," Irene said.

"I'm going to kill that sorry Mr. Dennihan," Jonathan said.

His mother looked at Jonathan. He thought she might say something about what he had just said. But then quickly she looked back down at Nobody and said, "We've got to get him home."

She stood and looked down toward the tiny general store just beyond the bus stop. "I can call Uncle Roy to see when he's coming," she said. "He'll come and we can. . . . You stay here with Nobody." She stood and started off rapidly toward the store with Ellen, but before they had gone more than a few yards they saw Uncle Roy's car. "Here he is! He left early for once. Thank goodness," she said.

Nobody yelped and tried to bite Uncle Roy but he got him in the back seat of the car anyway and Jonathan rode there with him and Ellen and their mother sat in the front but kept twisting around so she could look at Nobody. Jonathan watched the pain on her face. He read so much from her face, always.

They made a soft bed with quilts for Nobody beside the big oak tree. Uncle Roy went over to talk to Mr. Dennihan by himself. But he came back and said Mr. Dennihan was drunk and couldn't get him to make sense.

The next day Nobody's lower stomach was swollen and turned dark and he whimpered if Jonathan tried to touch him. Jonathan brought

Nobody little bowls of food and water but he wouldn't touch them. Once Jonathan got him to lick at the water but he didn't really drink any. Jonathan would go out and play and tried not to think about his dog. Then he would go back and speak to him and sometimes the dog cast his eyes up at Jonathan but he could hardly move his head anymore.

The first thing the second morning Jonathan went out and looked at Nobody but by then Jonathan didn't even like to look at him because he just didn't seem at all like Nobody.

Uncle Roy told their mother that the veterinarian he knew said there was nothing he could do. They could bring Nobody in and he would put him to sleep but they didn't want to do that and Ellen started crying when she heard them talking about whether to put him to sleep.

Late in the afternoon on the third day after Nobody was hit, Jonathan walked slowly over to the big oak tree to look at him. Jonathan spoke to Nobody but the dog did not move. Jonathan knelt beside him and reached his fingers out and touched the dog's face and started crying because Nobody was dead.

Jonathan ran to the kitchen to tell his mother. It was the only dog Jonathan had ever had and he cried about it and so did his mother and Ellen.

They buried Nobody, wrapped in the quilts he had lain on, high up on the field behind the clothes line.

David made a cross. He tried to drive the cross in the ground with a hammer. It would not go in the ground very well and his eyes filled up with tears so that he could hardly see what he was doing. All the while he kept hitting the cross harder and harder and crying absolutely silently.

Chapter Ten

Jonathan's father arrived from Washington two days after Nobody died.

His train came in close to nine that Sunday morning. He had been riding sitting up all night. Uncle Roy took Irene and the three Clayton children uptown to the dirty red brick and stone railroad depot that smelled of strong, soggy disinfectant that a porter used to mop the tile floor. Their voices echoed in the sparsely peopled, high-ceilinged station. They went outside to the tracks, stood around waiting for the train, and listened to their mother warn them about getting too close to the tracks. Then they all went back inside. Their mother bought them a package of assorted candy drops and David got the green one before Jonathan did. She told them to be quieter and they would walk back outside. Jonathan looked at her talking to Uncle Roy and realized for the first time that he was hardly as tall as she.

Irene was dressed in a white suit, and her eyes

sparkled. She kept talking to Uncle Roy, calling to them to be careful or quieter, and laughing. Uncle Roy came over smiling, his pipe drooping in his mouth, and gave each of them a penny to put on the railroad track. A freight train came in a few minutes and Jonathan could feel powerful rumble of the train in his stomach and legs and he could not stand there and watch the gigantic engine as it convulsed away without making a face, as if he had to squint to watch it. When it left, they got their pennies from around the tracks and laughed at how they were flattened to almost the size of a half dollar and were no thicker than a postal card.

They had been there for slightly more than half an hour when they heard the passenger train approaching. They watched the cars as they got slower and slower, the wheels making rhythmic, metallic bumps. Then it stopped and they looked back and forth and saw him get off a little ahead of them.

Their father waved and smiled broadly as their mother was waving back. They jumped up and down and Ellen tried to call to him above the noise of the train. He carried one suitcase and waved with the hand that held his cigar. They crowded around him and he hugged all three of them at the same time. Jonathan buried his face against his side and it was good to him to smell him again, the cigar, the slightly sweaty suit. Jonathan loved his father all over again and vowed he wasn't going to be embarrassed about him anymore ever.

They got in the car and were all talking at once. Their father laughed and tried to answer questions.

He sat in the front with Irene between him and Uncle Roy. Jonathan told him about Nobody but the sadness got washed away with other talk. He told them he had brought them just a little something that he would give them when they got to the house and he opened his suitcase.

As they pulled into the driveway, Jonathan half expected to see Nobody come bounding to greet them, and he glanced up to where the grave was. Then they were inside and David and Jonathan struggled with carrying the suitcase upstairs. They urged him to come on. He had stopped to hug Aunt Eva and to talk a moment. Then he came on up and Ellen, David and Jonathan stood around while he opened his suitcase. Aunt Eva had made Till and Cortland stay downstairs and they sulked about it in the library. Jonathan saw a pint whiskey bottle in the suitcase and saw his father wink at his mother. She smiled back and forth between the children and Joel. He gave each of the children four soldiers made of cast iron that sold for a nickel apiece. Then he realized that Cortland and Till were not upstairs so he called for them to come up also because he had brought them four soldiers each. Cortland acted bashful but Till did not. Till said she liked the soldiers even though they were for boys and that she was going to put them on her dresser and have them stand guard. Jonathan knew he would add his to the ones he kept in a scarred cigar box. Regularly he took his soldiers out by himself to have battles near the oak tree. There was a drama, with some variation, that he went through with the iron men. He always imagined himself as the one that was fitted out like a tough-faced Confederate soldier. The principal bad guy was a cowboy in a slouch hat who was about to draw his gun. Usually wounded rather grandly, the Confederate soldier would nevertheless always manage to win over the cowboy in the slouch hat.

Irene told them to go on outside and play because Joel wanted to take a bath and change clothes and that they would have an early lunch. She said Ellen could help her in the kitchen. Jonathan went outside and stood on the front porch, looking over toward Clown Mountain. The tree at the top swayed and laughed, bobbing its head down at the Dennihan pigpen house.

David came out and sat on the cement steps near where Jonathan stood.

"I sure am glad Daddy's home," Jonathan said, "and has a job and everything."

"Yeah. But this isn't home though, really."

"You know what I mean." Jonathan thought for a moment he might tell David that which he had told no one—how he had been ashamed of his father and embarrassed about him and how bad he had felt about it. Jonathan had watched his father carefully and listened to him when he came home, hoping there would be nothing that rekindled any feelings like he had been having. Jonathan was relieved that he did not feel the emotions that had bothered him so much; there wasn't, at that moment anyway, a disturbing trace of doubt about whether he loved his father. Jonathan pushed the old thoughts out of his mind. He wanted to speak of something pleasant and he decided against trying to explain it all to David anyway. "I wonder what it'll be like in Washington." Jonathan sat on the steps behind David.

"I don't know," David said. He sat with one foot thrown up on his opposite knee, rubbing his hand over his bare leg and studying it.

"What you doing?"

"Looking at my leg."

"Huh?"

"Looking at my leg."

Jonathan looked too and shrugged his shoulders. "What's the matter with it?"

"Nothing."

"Well then what're you looking at it for?"

David did not answer for a moment. "I'm not going to wear knickers to school in Washington. If I have to, I'm not going to school."

"What's the matter with knickers?"

"Nothing."

"Why aren't you going to wear the then? Practically everybody wears knickers."

"I'm getting too old." Then with a funny mixture of shame and pride, David said, "I need long pants now. I'm getting hair on my legs."

"Let me see." The dark, wavy, strangely foreign hair that signaled puberty was beginning to sprout. Jonathan marveled. David put his leg down and looked off embarrassed and whistled. Jonathan liked him very much as a brother then and felt a definite awe. "They'll get you some long pants, I'm sure,"

Jonathan said, trying to sound older himself. "Especially now that Daddy's got a job and everything."

Till walked up from the side yard carrying a handful of honeysuckle blossoms in one hand and her little glass vial in the other. The vial, as slender as a pencil, was about two and a half inches long. Tiny drop-by-drop she had been squeezing the nectar of honeysuckle blossoms into the glass vial. "I'm making my own bottle of honeysuckle perfume."

Jonathan watched her and even helped at times, but usually he would, after pulling apart the honeysuckle blossom, touch the drop to his tongue so that he contributed very little to the over-all production of her bottle of perfume, while nevertheless tasting a great deal of nectar.

After a while, Jonathan left Till and David talking on the front steps, and he strolled off into the yard. He stood plucking at one of the evergreen shrubs and decided to daydream about Charlotte, a girl who had been in his class. As far as Jonathan was concerned, she was the *only* girl in his class that spring. He would sit and watch her dark hair and long eyelashes and the teacher would call on him and he wouldn't know the place. Jonathan did have to admit to himself, however, that she was slightly on the plump side. For that reason, he was sure, during the class pageant she had been chosen to portray, not a raindrop or a beam of sunshine as she so very much wanted, but a full, ripe tomato.

Jonathan met her on the stairway after school when she had just found out about her role in the pageant. Almost on the verge of tears—and those wonderful long eyelashes!—she confessed to Jonathan the tragic thing that had happened, that she was a tomato and not a sunbeam. And indeed it did seem tragic to Jonathan, so he said something to her about that was all right and he reached out his hand and gently touched her shoulder. It was the first time he had touched a girl in an effort to show affection. Her shoulder felt stronger to him than he expected.

She looked up at Jonathan from underneath those eyelashes and he had never loved anyone so much in all his whole life. He told his mother about Charlotte's not getting the part and how she was almost crying and his mother shook her head sadly and said, "Children can get so very, very hurt in just one afternoon of their lives." His mother was always saying something dramatic and sad like that that stayed with Jonathan forever.

But Uncle Roy found out about Charlotte and several times asked Jonathan how his tomato was doing. Of course Jonathan hated him for it. Cortland said he didn't see anything wrong with tomatoes anyway, and kept on eating.

Jonathan's fantasies about Charlotte always had a dream-like suspension about them. She would come to him (an older Jonathan and a slimmer Charlotte) in need of comfort or help or consolation of some type and Jonathan, in his fantasies an aviator or something equally grand, would take her away from them, her tormentors, her detractors, the enemies of her happiness, and it gave Jonathan a wonderful feeling.

Aunt Eva called them to lunch and they ran around the side of the house and went into the kitchen. Their father, looking freshly bathed and smelling of shaving lotion, stood smiling and their mother kept standing near him. She looked pleased. The light lunch had grown into a sizable dinner and after they ate, Joel Clayton came out into the yard with Jonathan and the rest of them and stood around while they nudged each other for position to tell him of the things they had been doing and discovering and of Hubert and the hateful, dangerous, Mr. Dennihan. He promised he would walk down to the swimming hole after a short nap and he smoked his cigar and kept laying a hand gently on the tops of their heads. He said how tanned they were and how they had backs like velvet.

Late in the afternoon, their father went with them across the meadow to the swimming hole. Till and Cortland went with them and Jonathan carried Eureka that he showed to his father. Joel admired the swimming hole and said it was the best one he had ever seen, and he asked whose idea it was to use the burlap bags and David was very proud. Jonathan held the rock under water with one hand and showed him how easy it was to see.

Then suddenly they heard a scream coming from the Dennihan's house. It was hideously long and drawn out like the rending of a giant piece of cloth that kept going and going.

Ellen grabbed her father's hand when she heard it and they all stood still looking up at the pigpen house. Then they saw Mrs. Dennihan, followed quickly by Hubert, come almost tumbling out of the front door to the porch. They hesitated there a moment and then ran out into the yard, looking back at the front door.

Mr. Dennihan lurched into the doorway, stood there looking at them and they retreated farther onto the grassless front yard. The man and woman yelled something back and forth at each other and then he disappeared into the house.

It got quiet but Mrs. Dennihan and Hubert stayed in the yard until Mr. Dennihan appeared again and stalked down the rickety front steps of the porch and away from the house. He walked unsteadily down the dirt road toward the highway, his bandaged arm stuck out like a broken chicken wing.

Till said, "Don't you think you better say something to him, Uncle Joel, before he gets away?"

Joel shook his head, "It was just some sort of family fuss." But he looked worriedly back at Mrs. Dennihan and Hubert as they retreated slowly back into the house.

"He's mean," Ellen said.

"Let's not think about it," Jonathan's father said. "Let's think about something pleasant."

Jonathan hated that his father said that. It was just the kind of thing that Jonathan himself did without saying it; he switched to that which was pleasant, but he didn't want his father to do that. He wanted his father to go out there and straighten that Mr. Dennihan out once and for all. As they started back home, Jonathan glanced back at the Dennihan house and then up at Clown Mountain, and just as he suspected, the clown tree was swaying back and forth and nodding toward the Dennihan's.

Chapter Eleven

The next few days were lovely days, with their father home there with them and their mother not working. Mr. Thorn had gladly given her time off from the store. There were walks over the hills, the laughing joy of the swimming hole, and the soft grass of the evenings; then the long night meals with the comfortably heavy-voiced talk of adults going on into the night, the big soft, cool beds, and the early morning newness of everything outdoors.

Then one morning Jonathan killed a bird, and that was part of growing up.

And one afternoon he walked into the upstairs bathroom just as Till stepped out of the tub, and that was part of growing up.

The morning he killed the bird, he arose before anyone else. It seemed an enchanted time of day to Jonathan. He felt there was more promise then and a sweet loneliness that no other time of day could touch. The day was absolutely his and everything that was in it. It was a horrible time to kill a bird because it was as if he was god of the morning and he messed the whole thing up right off with killing a bird.

As he had walked through the silent house that morning, barefooted and wearing only a pair of short pants, he had no thought of taking David's gold-colored Daisy BB rifle outside. David was possessive about the rifle, Jonathan knew. But when he saw it leaning against the cardboard box on the back porch, he stopped, looked at it and picked it up. Jonathan tilted the gun up and down and heard the BBs rolling in the tube.

Outside he walked away from the house toward the cherry tree and the doll house that had not been used since Till was a little girl. He stood looking around him, holding the gun poised and feeling the power of being alone in the moist freshness of the day and holding the gun.

A drab, fat sparrow sat motionless in the cherry tree. Jonathan put the air rifle to his shoulder and almost casually pointed it at the bird and pulled the trigger. He felt the quick explosive burst of air push out the tiny BB and then the bird fell. It fell without a flutter and when it hit the ground it was with the deadest of all dead sounding little thuds. A lifeless little plop. Jonathan was startled. He hesitated a moment and then walked to where the bird had fallen. It lay on its side, hardly a feather out of place. Showing from the left side of its head was a droplet of blood, very red and thick. He did not want to touch the bird but he did and it was warm. He put it down and stood up. Then squatted again and looked

at the bird and wished like everything he had not
shot it. It hadn't been doing anything but enjoying
the morning too.

On the other side of the tree there were some
small bushes and he took a stick and scratched a
hole in the ground near them and put the bird in
and covered it up and then put some weeds over the
dirt. He felt terrible and promised God he would
never kill another bird. He ran back to the house
and put the rifle up and went around to the front
and sat on the steps until called to breakfast. His
mother wanted to know what was wrong and he said
nothing was wrong but he missed Nobody.

The next afternoon he had been playing outside
by himself when he went into the house to get a
spool he had with string wrapped around it. He ran
two steps at a time up the carpeted stairway, went to
his room and got the spool, and then decided to
make a quick trip into the large bathroom at the
head of the stairs. The door was pushed almost shut.
Jonathan shoved it open and started in.

Till gave a startled little cry. She stood in the
tub, half facing Jonathan, the afternoon sun from
the window streaming in on her wet skin. Jonathan
was as much shocked at first by finding her in the
bathroom as he was seeing her standing there naked.
He felt embarrassed but he stood as if he was
frozen, looking at her. He had not realized she was
so nearly a woman, a stranger; she did not seem like
the Till he knew at all. She looked delicate and
strong and grown up, all at the same time. He
looked at her white stomach and where her thighs

came together at the dark, coarse looking little patch of hair that still glistened from the bath. The sunlight sparkled on her small breasts.

It was really almost with a laugh, no annoyance at all, that she said, "Well . . . don't just stand there. Go on out."

Jonathan mumbled something about not knowing someone was in there, and Till laughed, rather gaily and not at all like herself and said, "Just please close the door on the way out."

Jonathan walked on outside and sat under the oak tree for a long time thinking about the way she looked. It was a strange thing and he felt very much alive and very happy. He went to find David to tell him what he had seen, but David wanted Jonathan to keep on describing it all in such detail that after a while it did not seem nearly as much of a happily magic thing to Jonathan as it had at first so he shut up about it.

It was during these summer days they made the sleds that would speed swiftly over pine needles.

Behind the huge garage, built on a hill with a half-story on top that was used mostly for storage, had been dumped three or four large plywood packing boxes. They discovered that pushing the packaging boxes through grass, weeds, and especially pine needles, the plywood quickly became slick.

David had the idea that they could build something in the shape of a sled and instead of separate runners, cover the bottom with the plywood and slide as fast over the pine needles as they could have had there been snow. They spent most of one afternoon sawing and hammering away at the project. They made one large enough for all five of them to sit on at one time if they sat on it like men on a bobsled. They carried it half way up the long hill behind the house to where the ground was lightly carpeted with pine needles.

They climbed on, grinning in anticipation, with David in front and Ellen on the rear. Gathering momentum slowly at first, it soon went sliding down the side of the hill at what seemed to them to be breathtaking speed. At the bottom, it slowed to a stop and they tumbled off laughing.

Although there was no way to steer the sled, this presented less of a problem than they thought at first. They found that the mounds of dirt near the base of most of the pine trees acted as a banking and turning device for the sled. When they picked out a likely looking run, they would send the sled off on an unoccupied silent trial run down the hill. Usually the mound of dirt was enough to make it swerve gently and miss the trees. Once or twice it was not and they had some repair work to do on the sled that evening.

Before they quit for the day, they vowed that the next day they would seek out the longest, most fun sled run they could find.

Before breakfast, Jonathan heard David outside hammering. Jonathan went out and helped him on the two smaller sleds he was making. When they went out later with the three sleds to seek the longest run possible, David ruled it would surely be found deeper in the pine woods to the right of the house. Aunt Eva fixed them a paper bag with five large cold biscuits stuffed with chunks of ham and another bag with purple grapes. Cortland had a small canteen filled with water attached to his belt.

They tramped through the hot, quiet woods in an angle away from the house, which was soon out of sight. After a while they came to a clearing in the woods, where they rested a moment. Looking back they could see they were right in line with the swimming hole and the Dennihan's pigpen house beyond. Even though they were still on their side of the highway, they were much closer at this point to the Dennihan's house than they were to their own because of the sharp turn the highway made.

Cortland wanted to know if they shouldn't go ahead and eat something now. David said to save it and they went on uphill with David leading the way, pulling one of the smaller sleds by its rope. Till and Cortland pulled the big one and Ellen and Jonathan took turns with the other small one. Their path kept angling back, while still going uphill, so they were soon in a position that actually put the Dennihan's house between them and their own.

Suddenly David, who was several yards ahead of them, called out. "Quick. Come here and look."

Letting go of the sleds, they ran up to him and could see before they got too close that he stood beside a large circular, cement-lined hole in the ground—an abandoned cistern, seven or eight yards across and close to ten feet deep.

Chapter Twelve

The bottom of the cistern was covered with almost a foot of pine needles. There were rusty tin cans in there also and some bottles, mostly unbroken—purple, brown, green and clear. It was as if someone had started to use the old cistern as a trash fill and then given up on the idea or moved away. It was a mysterious, somewhat awesome discovery for them, like stumbling across an Indian burial ground. Something that had been used and then abandoned so completely; something so forgotten, so secret. While Jonathan and the others looked at the cistern, David began to study the hillside up above them.

"Bad thing is," David said, "looks like it's right in the way of the best run we've seen." He pointed up the hill, which while sloping sharply upwards for twenty-five yards, ended abruptly by a steep cliff of rock. They pulled their sleds on up the hill, being careful around the edge of the cistern. When they got to the top of the hill, with the cliff at their backs, they looked down the hill they had climbed. It was like a long open gutter, with dense growth on each side.

From where they stood, the cistern presented a dangerous, gaping hole. There were only a few yards of open space on the left of the cistern, and the tangle of briars and thorns made a virtual wall except for this passage on the left side of the cistern.

"What do you think?" Cortland asked David.

David stood quietly, hands on his hips, studying the hill that stretched before them. "I don't know, exactly. It looks like a real good run—if we could miss that hole, that cistern, but . . ." and his voice took on the tone of the radio programs, ". . . if we hit it, it would mean sudden, sudden danger." He finished rather lamely on the word "danger," which Jonathan knew was not the one he started to use but "death" would have been a bit too dramatic, even for the radio program approach.

Then David dropped the pose and became again the practical and resourceful older brother. "If you look down there, there's a little bitty ridge that heads toward the hole. On this side of the ridge, I believe a sled will go in the cistern. But I think— don't know—that a couple of feet this way and it'll clear it and go sailing on down." Then, "Let's try it. We'll send down the two smaller ones first."

"I don't want to ride down there," Ellen said, pointing toward the cistern.

"Don't be stupid, Ellen," Jonathan said.

"We'll send them down empty," David said. "See?"

"Mother said not to call me stupid."

To follow David's sense of the dramatic, they lined the two smaller sleds up side by side, only a foot or two apart. They were aimed at slight angles away from parallel, with the expectation that one would go on each side of the faint spine that ran downward toward the cistern. David counted to three and they shoved the sleds. Almost silently the sleds sped down the slope, side by side for several yards, then the one on the left began a slight turn away from the cistern; the other, going straight as an arrow, covered the distance faster toward the hole, and with a slight leap right at the lip of the cistern, went over into it and crashed with a loud smacking sound against the bottom of the farther side.

"Wow," David said. "Lucky for us we weren't on that one."

"I wasn't about to get on it," Ellen said.

The other sled had missed the hole by a few feet and gone speeding down the hill for close to fifty yards. A beautiful run.

"We'd better try the big one, just to make sure," David said.

He placed it carefully to the left of the spine and sent it down. Just like the smaller one, it went toward the cistern at first and then began its soft turn away from it and on down the hill through the narrow clearing to the left of the cistern.

Laughing, they ran down toward the cistern, slowed to a cautious walk as they neared it and peered down. The first trial sled lay on its side, the front end banged up some but not as much as they had thought from the sound of it.

"We can use the ropes on the other two to lower me down there and get it," David said.

After he had sent the smaller sled up by the rope, David walked gingerly on the pine needles and around the broken bottles and rusty tins. He was getting ready to climb up the rope, but stopped. "Hey, let's use some of these bottles for target practice. For throwing at."

He tossed up fifteen or more bottles, which, after he had climbed back up the rope, they placed along the lip of the cistern and then went back to the rocky little cliff and loaded up with handfuls of rocks.

David made everyone stand behind a line he marked with his toe in the pine needles. They took turns throwing. David hit one of the bottles at a glancing blow and it fell over on its side. Till and Cortland missed completely. Jonathan threw and hit one dead center, exploding it so that shattered pieces of glass flew out from it. Ellen hit the ground in front of the bottles.

They took turns again and the performances were almost identical. On the third or fourth try David hit one of the bottles and knocked it backwards into the cistern. Jonathan only missed once and then he tipped the bottle so it rocked slightly. Cortland never hit one. He threw like a girl, bringing his arm down from over his head rather than from the side in line with the top of his shoulder.

"Golly, Jonathan, you ought to be a baseball pitcher," David said.

Jonathan smiled proudly at this praise from his

brother. He knew it was the one thing he could do better than David. "I don't like baseball," Jonathan said.

"He doesn't like to play on teams," Ellen said, repeating what Jonathan had told her.

"I've never seen anybody hit something so many times," Till said, tossing aside the one small rock she still held in her hand.

They decided to sit and rest and eat their ham biscuits and grapes before they made the sled run. Cortland passed his canteen around so everyone could take a sip.

Before they risked going down on the sleds themselves, they made one more test run, with the large one on the left of the ridge. It made the run perfectly.

Then they got ready to ride down on the big one. They were a little scared, a little nervous about it. David assured them that he would yell a warning if it looked like they were going toward the cistern and they could all jump in time.

He sat in front. Jonathan was on the end with Ellen in front of him. David told Jonathan to hold Ellen tight. Till sat right behind David.

"Okay, push," David said, and they gave the sled a shove with their hands. They picked up speed faster than they ever had before and they all held on to each other very tightly. Jonathan felt they were going right into the cistern but they began to veer to the left after a few yards and they went sailing past the left of the hole as fast as any sled on snow. The sled went on down the hill to a clearing and slowed to a stop when the hill gave out.

They were excited and happy and they tumbled off the sled, laughing.

They made many runs that day. They knew this was the best run they could find and at the end of the last trip down, Jonathan wanted to leave the sleds where they got off of them but David insisted they carry them back up the hill and hide them in thick bushes just behind where they started their run. The bushes grew just a few feet from the base of the cliff so that between the cliff and the bushes was a perfect hiding place.

"No one will find them there," David said.

"Heck, no one comes around here anyway," Jonathan said. But no, David would not have it that way. So each time they finished—and they rode the sleds many times in the next two days—they would pull them all the way back up the hill, walking carefully by the cistern, and hide them in the thick bushes at the foot of the cliff.

As they walked back to the house late that first evening and passed the clearing where they had stopped earlier in the day, Jonathan looked over across the highway and the meadow to the Dennihan's house. He saw the tiny figure of Hubert playing alone in the front yard. He was squatted in the dirt of the grassless front yard playing with a toy truck or car. For Jonathan, sadness as wispy as the haze of the evening descended on him and it was as if he wanted to call out to Hubert—and his voice would never have carried the distance that separated them—to say, yes, you can come play with us; yes, you can, you'd needn't play always alone.

But Till spoke up with the shrill, derisive tone she used at times, "There's ol' Hubert out in front of his pigpen. Ought to be in there with the pigs."

When she spoke, the sadness-tinged image of Hubert playing quietly alone disappeared and Jonathan could see Hubert with his thin, water-spattered legs and runny nose, the Hubert who knocked down their dam, and Jonathan was not at all sure how he felt about him.

He wished the Dennihans were not there to keep his feelings mixed up. Then, for a flicker of a moment, he felt the dread he had felt once or twice before—the dread that somehow they were not through with the Dennihans, and were being entwined with them, and he wanted to hurry up and move and get away from them.

Chapter Thirteen

They were finishing supper before Uncle Roy cleared his throat and started telling them about Mr. Dennihan. Even before he started talking, it was obvious to Jonathan that Uncle Roy had something on his mind and was waiting for things to settle down so he could tell them.

With only a few words, Uncle Roy had Jonathan and the others spellbound. "I've seen Mr. Dennihan drunk before but I've never seen him act as crazy as I did today. I think he would have killed Nick Fisher. Actually would have killed him. And then when Dennihan started running, it was like a dog having a running fit. He just kept at it." Uncle Roy held his cloth napkin and folded it and unfolded it and bobbed his head as he talked. He never used his hands when he talked and the folding and unfolding of the white napkin was a close as he came to accenting his words with gestures. But his face was unusually animated and he raised his sloping eyebrows.

He said, "I came into Charnock's store just when Nick Fisher had said something to Dennihan—something about his drinking, swilling it down like a pig—and Dennihan grabbed up a hammer handle from the shelf by the counter and swung as hard as he could. But Nick Fisher jumped back and the others grabbed Dennihan, and made him put the hammer handle down. Charnock told Dennihan to leave and he started to, but then he looked around at everyone like he didn't even know us. It was as if he was in a daze. He looked at everyone like he didn't know where he was."

Aunt Eva started to say something, as though to caution him against going into detail in front of the children.

With the slightest wave of his hand, Uncle Roy dismissed Aunt Eva's objection. "And Dennihan kept looking around from person to person as he started leaving. I don't think he even knew where he was. I know he had probably been drinking, but he wasn't all that drunk. It was something else. When he got outside, one of Charnock's dogs barked at him. They never bark at him and Dennihan went into a rage. He just bellowed at the dog. He sounded almost inhuman, like an animal himself."

Jonathan had stopped chewing, with a half-eaten bite of biscuit growing soggy in his mouth. He realized this and began to chew again and took a swallow of milk because suddenly his throat felt dry. He drank without taking his eyes off Uncle Roy. The part of about Mr. Dennihan sounding like an animal frightened Jonathan. It was like he was seeing a scary movie right at the table.

"When he yelled at the dog, the dog backed up some but kept on barking. Then Dennihan picked up a stick, an old tomato stake lying on the ground beside the store, and started chasing the dog. The dog ran behind the store and up toward those sheds of Charnock's and Dennihan ran after that dog. The dog ran around in circles and then headed across the field and Dennihan kept chasing him and yelling and waving the stick, with the arm he just got out of the sling flopping at his side. We couldn't hear what he was saying. It was mostly just yelling, I think."

Uncle Roy shook his head and took a delicate sip of his coffee. "We came outside and stood by the side of the store and watched him. He must have run as hard as he could for ten minutes or more. He fell down once or twice, and the first time someone in our group laughed just a little bit, sort of nervously, but then there wasn't any more laughing when Dennihan kept on running after that dog. The dog maybe thought he was playing because he stayed just out of Dennihan's range all the time. Darting this way and that."

Jonathan glanced at his mother, who was lightly biting her lower lip and looking very sad as she stared at Uncle Roy, listening intently.

"Finally, Dennihan stumbled across a log. He must have been two or three hundred yards away. He climbed up on the log and sat there, rocking back and forth and his shoulders were shaking." Uncle Roy must have realized how engrossed and animated he had become in the telling. He looked around and his manner calmed.

"From that distance, we couldn't tell whether Dennihan's shoulders were shaking from the running or whether—whether he was sitting there on that log in the middle of the field and crying."

Everyone around the table was quiet and hardly moved. Then, as if to break the spell, Aunt Eva said, "You just shouldn't stop by there. Charnock's store. It's getting so riff-raff hangs around there."

"Convenient," Uncle Roy said. "Visit with the boys."

Jonathan's mother said, "It sounds like to me, just like I said it would, that he's getting worse. A whole lot worse."

Uncle Roy took another little sip of his coffee and stared at his plate thoughtfully. "Some of them—Charnock and the rest—say the same thing. They say they've noticed a big difference in him in the past few weeks. He comes into the store when he's been drinking, which is just about all the time, and gets started on religion or Roosevelt and the Depression and won't be quiet about it. He starts talking all sorts of irrational rot."

"Well, he's always been religious," Aunt Eva said, "in a primitive sort of way."

"He's not talking religion. Just a lot of gibberish," Uncle Roy said. "Some of them are even saying Dennihan ought to be in the state hospital."

Jonathan's father, who had seemed lost in thoughts of his own, said, "I wonder where he's getting all the money for whiskey?"

"No telling," Uncle Roy said. "Borrowing a little

here, selling something there. Probably drinking white lightning. Can get that cheap."

"Yes," Aunt Eva said in a scolding tone, "probably right there at Charnock's."

"Lightning?" Ellen asked.

"It's the name of . . . of a whiskey . . . a homemade whiskey," their mother said.

"Well, let's just change the subject," Aunt Eva said. "I don't think this is the healthiest kind of conversation for little pitchers."

"Yeah, we've got big ears," Ellen said, and even Uncle Roy laughed.

A little later their mother said, "I feel sorry for the little boy, and the woman, too, but really the little boy."

Jonathan thought about it and felt sorry for Hubert, also, and wished he wouldn't keep thinking such bad things about Hubert and then he tried to put it out of his mind.

Just before everyone was about ready to get up from the big kitchen table, where the talk had drifted from the Dennihans to the Depression to Roosevelt, their mother said, "You haven't had much to say tonight, Joel." She lightly touched his arm.

"Yes, well. . . ." His voice trailed off, along with a faint, almost pathetic attempt at a smile that faded and trailed as his voice did. Jonathan knew his father was very uncomfortable and he watched him as he fumbled unwrapping a cigar.

It got very quiet. It was as if everyone knew to be quiet. Then his father looked up from the cigar at everyone looking at him and he took in everyone with his eyes, one at a time. Very softly, for there was no need to speak loudly in the hush, he said, "Little pitchers or no, I've got something to say. Maybe I shouldn't say it with everyone at the table, but we're about through and I want to get it over with."

"Well what in the world?" Aunt Eva said.

His father held the cigar tightly and both of his hands were on the table. He glanced at their mother and then looked straight ahead. "I don't think I have the job in Washington."

"Don't have it?" Aunt Eva said.

"No." He looked at their mother, who sat there staring at him and not speaking.

"But I thought. . . ." Aunt Eva's voice faded.

It was quiet. Jonathan did not want to look at Till or Cortland.

"I thought so too." He looked at their mother again. "I really did. The way they talked and everything. I thought for sure I had it. They were supposed to give me a definite answer the day I was to come down here. But they stalled it off."

Joel continued fumbling with his cigar. "And then they told me that they'd let me know for sure by letter or phone down here within a couple of days or so. I've written them but they haven't answered."

Softly he said, "That's been more than a week, almost two. I haven't wanted to admit it until the last possible moment, but now, now it looks like for sure. . . ."

Uncle Roy spoke evenly, the lawyer's voice:

"But isn't it still possible, just possible, that you may get positive news?"

"Well, there's always a possibility, I guess."

"Oh, Joel," their mother said in a voice that was almost a soft cry. "Why didn't you say something sooner? Why didn't you let me know?"

"Because . . . because everyone was so happy. Everyone was so happy. Talking about Washington. And I just kept hoping that each day, each day something would happen. I would hear. But now. . . ."

Jonathan could see his father's jaw muscles moving.

Irene looked very, very tired. And she sat there and looked at their father and then down at her plate. "Children," she said, "go on outside and play."

"We haven't had any dessert," Cortland said.

"Go on outside," Aunt Eva said sharply.

Till and Cortland got up and promptly started outside, but David stood close to their father. "Are we going to stay here?" he asked. David seemed grown up to Jonathan.

"I don't know yet, David." He touched David's arm lightly. "But don't worry."

Their mother quickly raised her head, her chin lifted a little proudly and made the smile come back. "Don't you children worry. Something will turn up." She moved her hands as if to wave away any doubts. "Why . . . why this job may come through after all. Who can tell? Who can tell?" But her voiced trembled ever so slightly at the end.

Uncle Roy said, "This is Thursday. I'd wait until Monday and then, by George, I'd call them up. Call

them up collect. Find out something. You have a
right to expect decent treatment from them. Maybe
you're being premature in this."

"Yes, maybe."

"One way to look at it, Joel," Aunt Eva said, "is
while you may not have the job, it's true, you don't
not have it either."

His father stared at Aunt Eva rather blankly.

"What I mean is, so, there is some hope, actually. Yes, there is. There definitely is."

Ellen tugged at Jonathan's arm. "Come on outside. They want us to go play."

They went outside but they didn't play. They
mostly just stood around. Jonathan looked up at
Clown Mountain and the Dennihan place and hated
being here in the mountains.

He went over to the roots of the big oak tree
where Nobody had died and sat there by himself.
He hated the way his father was, the way he didn't
have a job and wasn't in charge of everything. Or,
really, not in charge of anything. He almost said to
himself that he hated his father but then the feelings
got all mixed up and he would only say the he hated
the way his father was and the way he fumbled with
his cigar at the table and looked at everyone. He
hated that his father's jaw muscles were moving.
And he was ashamed, and then he hated himself,
too.

Ellen walked up and stood by Jonathan.
"What's the matter?"

"Nothing." He did not look up at her but he
could see her bare feet and little legs. Then he knew

what it was he really felt. It was that he felt sorry for all of them. Yes, he felt sorry for all of them, for Ellen with her bare feet and little girl legs, and, yes, he even felt sorry for his father, and it was all he could do not to let Ellen see that he was crying.

Chapter Fourteen

Later, Jonathan and the others sat in the library with the adults for a while before they had to go up to bed. Their father sat on one end of the couch and their mother next to him.

Jonathan would not look at his father. David, who was unusually quiet, sat at the other end of the couch. Uncle Roy fussed with his newspaper more than he read it and Aunt Eva was on her second cup of coffee, cigarette held elegantly in her ivory holder. Jonathan and the others were scattered about the floor and in and out of chairs. Cortland had his head up against the radio which Aunt Eva had made him turn low. Their father felt in his shirt pocket, pulled out matches, and then got up to go into the kitchen to get his cigar.

"Nervous," Aunt Eva said softly to their mother, nodding her head in the direction their father had gone.

"Yes, he is."

"Well, I simply don't know what we're all going

to come to. What this country is going to come to if we don't get out of this Depression."

Their mother said, "People keep saying it's getting over. That Roosevelt is getting us over it, but I haven't noticed."

Uncle Roy spoke to his newspaper, "The only thing Roosevelt is getting us is into a war. Then the Depression will be over."

"Oh, we're not going to war, Roy."

"Yes, we are."

"When?" David asked.

Their mother said, "He's just talking. Now don't you worry. We're not going to war."

Uncle Roy shook his head and kept on looking at the paper.

Their father came back into the room. After he sat down, he spoke with forced brightness: "Tomorrow I think I'll go into town and see if I can find something. There's bound to be something here."

"Very few jobs here," Uncle Roy said. "Very few."

"Maybe Mr. Thorn would give you something," their mother said. "Just something for a while until we can sort of get on our feet."

"Yes, why not?" Aunt Eva said.

"I think he's having a hard time just paying you, Irene," Uncle Roy said. "Of course, I don't want to sound pessimistic. Just practical. Just reasonable. Still think the best thing to do is wait until the first of the week and see—and call them, in Washington. Of course, if you want to see Thorn, I'd wait until just before closing on Saturday. When he's through for

the week and taken in as much money as he's going
to for the week—and hasn't paid it all out yet."

Relighting his cigar, their father said, "That's
what I'll do. Saturday afternoon I'll just go in to see
Mr. Thorn. And tomorrow, tomorrow I'll just. . . ."

Their mother filled the silence with, "Tomorrow, why don't you take the children fishing. To
Mattaskeet Lake."

Ellen scrambled onto his lap with joy. Even
Jonathan, who stayed a little back behind the others,
was pleased but tried not to show it too much.

"Yes," their father said, smiling, "that's what
we'll do. We'll go fishing." He laughed out loud.
When in doubt—and down and out—just go
fishing. Yes, that's the thing."

Uncle Roy smiled faintly at their father and then
went back to the paper.

Probably because of Uncle Roy's glance, as if
seeing his father through other eyes, Jonathan
suddenly thought his father looked rather silly,
sitting there grinning with a cigar in his mouth and
no job. Jonathan began all over again to wish his
father acted more like a judge or something and
looked stern and knew exactly what was practical
and reasonable. But then Jonathan began reluctantly
to give way to happiness, to the thought of getting
up early to go fishing, and the early-morning excitement of it.

They went to bed talking about going fishing.
Jonathan could hear the soft murmur of the adults
talking downstairs just before he went to sleep, and
he began to dream during the night and it was a bad

dream that left him with a feeling of terror and depression. In the dream, his father and mother were standing in a room, maybe a school room, and Jonathan and David and Ellen stood behind their mother and father as people walked by and looked at them, and Jonathan knew they were not dressed nearly as well as the other people there, and he felt out of place and ashamed, but his father was smoking a cigar and joking with someone. Then the dream changed and Jonathan was running away from Mr. Dennihan with Nobody, and Jonathan knew in the dream that Nobody was dead, but Nobody was there with him anyway, and they got right to the screen door on the back porch and Jonathan couldn't get the screen door open. Then the screen door turned into a thick, heavy solid wooden door that he knew he would never get open. Mr. Dennihan kept getting closer and making a scary animal sound.

Jonathan sat straight up in the bed. He knew he made some kind of noise, a cry or sob. He heard David stirring in the other bed, but maybe he didn't wake up. Jonathan lay back and made himself thinking about going fishing and how much fun that will be.

Chapter Fifteen

The next morning David woke Jonathan a few minutes past five. David had already dressed and slipped downstairs to see the clock in the living room. Jonathan got dressed and then they tiptoed into their mother's and father's room. They were still asleep. Their father lay on his back and their mother on her side with an arm across his chest. David touched his father's shoulder; he opened his eyes and looked puzzled, then smiled at them. He eased out of bed but their mother woke up anyway and mumbled to have fun and be careful. His father patted her gently on her rear, then whispered for Jonathan and David to wake the others while he fixed breakfast. Jonathan told him he wasn't hungry but that didn't do any good.

While Ellen, Cortland and Till were getting dressed, David and Jonathan went out to the back side of chicken house and dug fat and healthy looking earth worms. In the first light of the morning they could see it was going to be a beautiful day, and by the time they carried the can of worms back toward the house they could smell the sausage and streak-a-lean their father was cooking.

After they had eaten and had all the fishing poles ready to go, they had to stand around for what seemed to Jonathan for another eternity while Cortland went to the bathroom again. Ellen got the hiccups while they waited and their father took her back into the kitchen and made her drink nine swallows of water, and David said that now *she'd* probably have to go to the bathroom before they could ever get started.

Jonathan thought they were going to borrow Uncle Roy's car to ride, but David and their father wanted to walk. It was a good two miles to Mattaskeet Lake, dammed up more than a hundred years earlier for a grist mill operation which had long since ceased. Now it had a golf course at the far end, but there where they fished it was as wild and remote as it had been in the beginning. Most of the trip would lead them along Mattaskeet Road.

The walk was pleasant there in the silvery morning and they all talked and laughed. Jonathan found himself hardly thinking at all about his father's not having a job; he couldn't decide whether to make himself think about it and be sort of mad at his father, or just go along and let the good feelings of going fishing wash over him.

Although David stayed close beside their father, Jonathan and Ellen would often scoot ahead or lag behind, or dart to this side or that, but always come back to walk with them.

Till walked along rather primly, Jonathan thought. Walking along there that morning, wearing old shorts and shirt, her fishing clothes, she seemed like a different person from the one Jonathan saw standing in the bathtub with the sunlight glistening on her. In fact, he had a difficult time accepting that it had really happened.

Till surprised Jonathan by saying, "Why're you staring at me?"

Jonathan felt his face redden. "I'm not. Least, didn't mean to. I mean looking, staring."

Till appeared ready to say something else. Then a slight smile crept along the corners of her lips. "I guess you're kind of all right, Jonathan—even if you are picky with your food."

He grinned at her. Then she turned her head and continued walking, but the little smile was still there.

Ellen walked beside their father and tugged at his hand. She looked up and asked him, as she often did their mother, "Do you love us?"

Their father beamed and said, "Oh, yes." He kept looking down at Ellen as they walked. He held her hand and a moment later said, "You children will never know just how much your mother and I *do* love you until you have children of your own." He paused. "Then you'll know."

"Of my own?" Ellen said. "That'll be a long time."

"Yes, but when you do you'll remember what I said. You'll see."

Toward the end of the walk they had to go

single-file up the narrow path that led along the edge of the bank through the woods to the clearing where they fished. Walking through the path Jonathan could smell the vegetation's dampness, and then when they got into the clearing, with the sun hitting on it, he could smell the pine needles and the water.

Their father was the last one to get started fishing because he had to help Ellen bait her hook and he had to help Cortland get his line untangled. After inspecting Jonathan's line, he wanted to know where Jonathan's lead sinker was.

Jonathan said he liked to fish without one, and let the worm sink slowly. Jonathan would stretch the line out on the ground behind him and whip the pole over his head and send the line out. The cork would plop on the water and the hook would lay out on the water and start to sink, slowly taking the line slicing gently through the water.

They started catching small perch or bream right away. They had been fishing for about an hour when Jonathan whipped his line out and no sooner had the cork settled than it went streaming out of sight. Jonathan tugged sharply and then half-ran backwards from the lake. He stumbled once and could feel the sharp tug of the fish on the other end of the line. The tip of his pole bent downward as the fish fought against him. But Jonathan held on and began to back up, pulling the fish out onto the bank, where it flopped wildly on the pine needles. To Jonathan, the fish looked huge. All he had ever caught before were bream. This was a largemouth bass. The largest fish he had ever caught. Jonathan danced with glee.

But actually, according to the notches David had carved an inch apart on his pole, the fish was a trifle less than ten inches long—the legal limit.

Their father measured the fish carefully over again. Now Jonathan stood still, holding his breath.

"He's not ten inches long," Till said scornfully. "You're not supposed to keep him."

With the fish held carefully with both hands up against the pole, their father kept studying the fish.

Jonathan's heart began to sink and he couldn't say anything.

With the cigar clutched in his teeth, Jonathan's father looked up at him and managed a secret little smile; then he took his thumb and forefinger and grabbed the fish's lower jaw and pulled its mouth open. He stretched the fish's lower lip until it brushed the ten-inch mark. "There!" he said triumphantly.

"But you stretched his mouth way out," Till protested. "Practically pulled his mouth out of joint!"

Holding back a chuckle, Joel said, "Now, Till, if you were High Judge of the Whole Universe, which would you think would be the best thing to do—to stretch a big fish's mouth a bit or shrink a little boy's heart?"

Till puffed out a breath of air, sighed and said, "Aw, let him keep the dumb ol' fish."

Jonathan was pleased but he didn't jump up and down about the fish. He kept squatting there on the ground beside his father.

Jonathan had watched his father's hands while

he worked on stretching the fish's mouth and Jonathan had looked up closely at his father's face just before he had spoken to Till. He had studied his father's face and he kept looking at him. It was as if for the first time, suddenly, Jonathan saw his father and saw him more than he had ever seen him before. It was a strange feeling for Jonathan. A revelation that he wasn't expecting. He had looked at his father's hands while he pulled on the fish's mouth and had seen the veins in his hands and the little stubble of hair on the backs of his hands and how one fingernail was broken a bit, and he saw the texture of his father's skin as closely as he saw the texture of his own. He had looked at his father's face and seen how he had not shaved that morning and there was a very slight growth of beard, with silver mixed in with the darker colors. He saw the creases around his eyes when his father looked up at Till. And most of all Jonathan saw his father as a person, a separate person, and saw him for the first time as someone he knew, like he knew David or someone maybe at school back at their old home, someone close to him; Jonathan was very moved by it. It was as if in that moment he could feel everything his father had been feeling and going through to try to make things work and to make them happy.

He caught Jonathan's look and paused and then smiled and put his hand on Jonathan's shoulder. Then they got up and didn't look at each other and got busy putting the fish on a separate stringer from the others.

They fished until close to noon but the fish had stopped biting about eleven except for a small perch or two. They walked back and it seemed much farther and later in the day than it was. Jonathan walked close to his father and carried his fish proudly on its separate stringer. Till made several comments about the fish but Jonathan was too happy to be bothered by her.

When the fish was cleaned, though, along with the rest, it didn't look so large and then when it was cooked it got even smaller and Jonathan didn't want to eat it anyway.

Chapter Sixteen

On Saturday afternoon, their father bathed and shaved and put on his suit in preparation to going to see Mr. Thorn about a job. He told Jonathan and the others that they could not go with him, that he was sure it would be best if he went alone. It was easy for Jonathan to see that he didn't want to go at all; he smiled so much and talked so light-heartedly, all the while pacing around the house.

Uncle Roy had given him the car keys and then Joel laid them absently on the kitchen table and when he got to the car, he discovered he didn't have them. He came back into the kitchen for the keys and gave their mother another light peck of a kiss But he was frowning so much she made him kiss her again.

He went back out of the kitchen and on the way knocked the ashes from his cigar against the door jamb on the back porch and muttered about that. He mashed the ashes with the toe of his shoe, which was not polished quite as well as it should have been.

The car didn't start immediately and when it did he jerked it getting it moving and Jonathan saw that he was frowning as he drove away.

Jonathan, Ellen and David stayed around their mother. She kept suggesting they go out to play. David asked her twice when she thought their father would be back and whether she thought he would get the job from Mr. Thorn. She told him not to worry, that everything would work out fine.

A little later their mother sat in the library with Aunt Eva and Uncle Roy, talking. Jonathan, David, and Ellen wandered into the library, also, appearing to be at loose ends. David sat close to their mother. He seemed to be listening to the conversation more closely than Jonathan and Ellen.

Their mother was saying, ". . . but you'll have to admit, Roy, that it seems that things, events, have just worked against him ever since we went to Georgia."

Aunt Eva broke in to say, "Well, goodness knows, he's my brother and I love him dearly, but when it comes to practical things, well, he's such a dreamer."

"Just doesn't face facts," Uncle Roy said.

"And, Irene," Aunt Eva said, "you'll remember that things—or events, as you say—were really not going well before you went to Georgia."

"He's got to be more decisive and take the bull by the horns," Uncle Roy said. "He can't just keep vaguely hoping things are going to happen for his benefit."

Their mother acted as though she was going to say something else. But before she could, David suddenly stood up. He stood by the couch, his arms straight down by his sides, his fingers held stiffly against his legs. For an instance, his throat worked but he didn't utter a sound. Then he said, with startling loudness, "Don't talk about my Daddy!" He glared at Uncle Roy and then at Aunt Eva and back at Uncle Roy. "Don't do it," he said. His voice trembled as if he might be close to tears but he surely didn't sound put-on to Jonathan like one of his charters on the radio. It was all David, spoken loudly and forcefully. "You've said enough bad things about him, and they're not true. They're not true."

Their mother tried to tell him that it was all right, that nothing was meant by it, that they all loved his daddy.

Then Uncle Roy stood up and faced David, who remained almost motionless, except that his shoulders trembled just a little. For several seconds Uncle Roy looked at David, studied him as if David had just that moment walked into the house. Then Uncle Roy said softly, "The boy is right." He looked at David a moment longer then turned and started out of the room, but he stopped and faced David again. "I'm proud of you," he said and left the room.

David breathed out and let his shoulders relax so they didn't tremble anymore. He looked around a bit embarrassed and mumbled that he thought he'd go on upstairs. Irene got up and followed him. Aunt Eva looked like she was going to say something to her but she was already out of the room. They were all very quiet. Then Aunt Eva said gaily, "Turn the radio up, Ellen, my dear. Let's hear what's on the radio."

Later on when their father drove up and slowly got out of the car they could tell right away that he didn't get a job.

It was quiet and rather strained that Saturday afternoon. After supper their father walked out in the front yard with David and they talked for a while. Jonathan stood around on the front porch and watched them, and he looked up at Clown Mountain and the tree was perfectly still. He glanced at the miniature pigpen house and thought he saw Hubert come out on the rickety little front porch and stand there a moment and then go back inside.

Their father rubbed a hand across David's shoulder and smiled at him. Then he said something and patted David's shoulder again and walked around the side of the house toward the rear. David stood by the big oak tree looking out across the meadow.

Jonathan acted like he wasn't walking anywhere in particular and strolled to where David stood. David looked at him but didn't say anything. They talked a minute or two about the swimming hole. Then Jonathan blurted out, "I love Daddy, too."

David looked at him, and then said almost angrily, "Of course you do!"

"No sense in getting mad about it."

"I'm not mad."

"You sound like it."

"I'm not." Then David softened a bit. "Didn't mean to."

They stood awkwardly around a few moments and then Jonathan said, "Well, I just wanted to say it." He didn't look at David.

David said simply and rather quietly, "He's our daddy."

Jonathan felt better but he didn't want to show it too much, so he was relieved when David poked at him and said, "Let's go catch some light'ing bugs."

To Jonathan everything seemed a lot better and the good feeling washed over him as they chased around after the fireflies.

Later that night when they were getting ready for bed, their mother was in the room alone with Jonathan while the others were getting washed up. Jonathan had been waiting so he could tell her. "David's not the only one who loves Daddy. I do, too."

She looked at Jonathan kindly, a hint of a smile in her eyes.

Since she didn't say anything right away, Jonathan was at a loss. "I just wanted to say that," he said. "That I love Daddy, too."

He was embarrassed because it suddenly seemed to him that what he was saying didn't make a whole lot of sense since he'd never said he didn't love his father. How was anybody supposed to know what some of the things were he had been thinking? He was beginning to feel almost miserable and maybe he shouldn't have said anything at all.

But then his mother said, "I know you do, Jonathan." She said it quietly and kept looking at him like she could read all the things he had been thinking about this father, and she reached over and patted his knee.

"I don't even care if he doesn't have an ol' job," Jonathan said.

She smiled brightly again and began to pick up the things David had dropped on the floor before he went to the bathroom. "But it'd make it nicer if he had a job," she said and smiled directly at Jonathan. "No question about that." Then she stood and looked out the window toward the cemetery a minute, folding David's short pants in her hands. She turned back to Jonathan, who sat there on the edge of the bed watching her. "Sometimes you think it'd be the easiest thing in the world not to love someone. Then everything would be easier . . . you could just not care." She paused a moment, "But that's not the way we are."

Ellen came squealing into the room with David right behind her, trying to pop her rear with a towel. Irene tried to get them quieted down and ready for bed.

Their father came upstairs to tell them good-night. He rubbed their backs, each one of them separately, and said, as he always did, "Like velvet." He kissed them on top of their heads, and Jonathan could smell the familiar, comforting odor of cigar that lingered on him, so much a part of him.

Jonathan felt better, more grown up, and he said to himself, yes, he did love his father and that was that; that was a commitment and there would be no more of the other.

Chapter Seventeen

Sunday was a quiet day. During the afternoon, Jonathan, David, and Ellen went for a rather solemn walk with their mother and father. It was cloudy that day and the wind picked up. By nightfall the wind blew hard, as it does in the mountains, and Jonathan went to sleep listening to the wind. He thought about how it must blow through Hubert's rickety house.

Some time during the night it rained but by early morning the sun was out and the wind had stopped blowing. Uncle Roy had eaten early on Monday morning and gone to work. The rest of the family sat around the kitchen table. Jonathan knew that their father was going to call Washington later in the morning and they would be told to go on outside then; but they stayed as long as they could. It was already after nine-thirty.

Jarringly loud, the phone rang. Aunt Eva picked up her cigarette and said her usual, "Now I wonder who that could be?" She went into the dining room to answer it and came back quickly. No one had spoken while she was gone. "It's long distance for you, Joel."

He glanced quickly at their mother, set his chin firmly and walked into the dining room to answer the phone. Their mother sat rigidly in the chair at the kitchen table, staring toward the window near the refrigerator.

Then, from what they could hear, they could tell that after a minute it was pleasant and their mother and Aunt Eva dared to look at each other. Their eyes permitted the sharing of the slightest trace of hopeful smiles.

Joel talked loudly and jovially toward the end of the conversation. When he finally hung up and came back into the kitchen, he grinned and rubbed his hands together happily. He had already unwrapped a cigar and he fumbled for a match. "A match, a match," he said, almost laughing.

Imitating his happy tone, Aunt Eva said, "Here, here," handing him one of the wooden kitchen matches.

"What, Joel? What . . ." their mother said, smiling too.

He sat down, grinning at her. He touched her hands, which lay on the kitchen table. "I've got it!" Triumphantly. "I've got it. Not in Washington. But listen to this." He leaned back and spread his hands before him, cigar clinched jauntily in his teeth. "Right here in the state. North Carolina. Working out of Raleigh. I'll be the North Carolina and Virginia representative."

"Oh, that's even better. Just wonderful," she said and got up and leaned over and kissed him lightly.

Grinning still, he swatted her rear. "They hadn't called," he said, "because there was a big shuffle. They were apologetic about that. Not calling. Real apologetic. Said they made some last minute changes when the Washington man they thought was retiring decided to stay on. Another quit for another job, and, well, anyway, the North Carolina and Virginia territory opened up. Working with just schools and libraries."

"Schools and libraries. That'll suit you fine," Aunt Eva said. "I'm going to call Roy at the office. He'll be so happy for you."

Joel donned a more serious, businesslike manner. "Got to go to Washington in a week for a few days' orientation, as they call it, at their expense, and start to work in two weeks. Two weeks from today . . . I start to work." He became the beaming child-man again. "We've got to get a place to live. Oh, we've got a lot to do—but isn't it, isn't it grand?"

"Roy will help you, help you financially get settled, as he said," Aunt Eva said.

"We'll be leaving here in . . . ?" their mother said.

"Just a day or so. Oh, we've got a lot to do." His cigar had gone out. "A match. A match. Another match," he laughed.

They all talked about the job and moving but staying in North Carolina. Ellen had a hard time understanding that Raleigh was the capital of the state and Washington was the capital of the country and that the District of Columbia was not a state. Jonathan didn't help much because he kept getting it mixed up in trying to explain it and their mother got after him for calling Ellen dumb but she wasn't angry.

Jonathan felt wonderful about everything. It all seemed so good that he felt like he ought to think about something else, just to take the intense focus away from the job and moving and all. But he couldn't. And at the same time he had difficulty really and truly imagining what it would be like, with a house of their own again and his father working and Jonathan not being ashamed; then Jonathan told himself he wasn't ashamed anyway, and had already decided that. Just the same, this, whatever it was, was going to be so much better. He breathed deeply and exhaled slowly and smiled and felt like he would burst.

Outside, Jonathan and the others stood around on the front porch laughing and talking about going swimming after lunch. Jonathan felt so swelled up with being happy he said expansively, "Heck, why don't we tell ol' Hubert he can use the swimming hole if he wants to?"

"Why not?" David said, smiling and slapping Jonathan on the back as if they were both grown men. Then David apparently remembered that Till and Cortland were not moving at all, that they would still be there to use the swimming hole. "If that's all right with you and Cortland," he said.

She shrugged. "Why not?" Then she looked at David and said, "It seems like you all have already moved. And it won't be any fun with you all gone."

For the first time Jonathan realized the news wasn't all happy for everyone, and he saw the softness in Till's eyes, and she kept looking at David and looking away. But then, after a silence of a few moments, Till spoke, and sounded like herself. "Sure. We might as well tell him he can use it. No sense in us being a stinker just because he is. We won't be using it with you all gone. Besides, the summer'll be gone before long, anyway."

"Yeah," Cortland said.

Jonathan felt the sudden brush of sadness, like something damp, when Till said the summer will soon be gone.

"Okay, we will then," David said. He looked over the valley toward the Dennihan's. "And Mr. Dennihan's not there. His truck is gone."

At that time they had no way of knowing that the night before, Dennihan's truck had broken down at Charnock's store and Dennihan, clutching two quart Mason jars of clear whiskey, had walked home, stopping every hundred yards or so to take a swig from one of the jars.

Chapter Eighteen

Lunch was later than usual. They had all waited for Uncle Roy to come home from the office for lunch, which was unusual for him, but he was to take their mother and father back downtown with him. Their mother was going to see Mr. Thorn and pick up what little money he owed her, and, more importantly, the dolls she had dressed that had not yet been sold. Their father was going with Uncle Roy to look at some used cars. Uncle Roy knew of a Ford that could be bought at a good price, but their mother said she thought Fords were tinny and that a Plymouth would be better.

After lunch Jonathan and the others waited on the front porch for a period of time, at Aunt Eva's insistence, to let their food digest before they went to the swimming hole. They had not told the adults about their plans to give Hubert permission to use the swimming hole. Finally she came to the door and told them they could go on down to the creek. She told them to be careful and not to stay too long.

She said she was going to take a nap because it was hot and there had been a lot of excitement.

The heat had made Jonathan and the others a little drowsy; they had sat there and looked up at the very blue sky and high white puff clouds and listened to the patterned whirring of insects. They had almost given up on the idea of going over to tell Hubert. Then David said they ought to get going. They did not have the washtubs but out of habit Jonathan clutched the stone Eureka in his right hand. He wore a faded pair of blue short pants he used for a bathing suit; Cortland and David also had on short pants. Till wore a dull orange bathing suit and Ellen had on her navy blue itchy-looking wool one that had a tiny hole on the right hip.

They walked diagonally across the front yard and through the open place in the high hedge, then across the road and the meadow to the creek. Jonathan made a lazy attempt at catching a grasshopper on the way, and David threw a rock at a lizard that had been sunning itself. They stopped for a moment at the swimming hole. The water was bright and clear. Jonathan looked up at the tree on Clown Mountain. The tree was still. He looked at Dennihan's house.

"Doesn't look like anyone's around," David said.

"Probably inside," Jonathan said.

"Maybe taking a nap."

"He doesn't take any nap, I'll bet," Cortland said.

"We might as well, I guess, go on up there,"

David said. "We said we were going to tell him."

Till shrugged.

They went at an angle away from the creek to the rutty little dirt road that led upward another hundred and fifty yards to the house. Everything stood out clearly to Jonathan, every patch of weeds, the way a slight breeze bowed the top of a dusty bush beside the road, the rocky and gutted road itself and always the soft, whirring flutter of insects.

The pigpen house looked even dirtier and more rickety as they got closer. It began to look greasy to Jonathan and he could imagine he smelled the kerosene that was surely used for heat. Except for their footsteps and the insects it was very quiet. Jonathan looked behind him and thought how Uncle Roy's house looked farther away than he thought it would.

Ellen took hold of Jonathan's left hand; he still carried Eureka in his right. Over the top of the pigpen house, right in line with them, was the small peak of Clown Mountain, but up as close as they were the tree lost a great deal of its clown-like shape; it became just another tree but it still bothered Jonathan. It was as if everything in him was drawn real tight. He thought he felt Ellen shudder just a little bit. He was almost wishing they hadn't decided to come.

"Doesn't look like anyone is home," David whispered. His whisper sounded loud in the still-ness.

They were within twenty-five yards from the front of the house. As they got even closer Jonathan was certain he could smell the kerosene and the dampness, like rotting wood and discarded dishwater. The smell hung in the air. Near the dilapidated front steps there was a small metal blue and red toy dump truck with its wheels missing. The roof the truck's cab had all of its paint rubbed off so metal was shiny, as if it got that way by Hubert's pushing it along in the dirt on its top.

They paused in front of the porch steps, standing in a tight little bunch and stared at the crumbly looking screen door. There wasn't a sound.

"I guess we'll just knock," David whispered. "Come on."

They followed closely up the steps. Jonathan could see through the front screen door to the bright rectangle of light that was the back door. But his eyes were not accustomed to the dimness inside.

David took a breath and knocked lightly and the screen door shook and echoed the sound. Then it was quiet for a second.

Suddenly, Ellen dug her fingers into Jonathan's arm and made a deep moaning sound in her throat.

The sound she made terrified Jonathan. He snapped his head to look. She pointed over to the side of the yard just at the edge of the porch.

Hubert lay on his stomach, arms and legs thrown out at angles as if he were still running. The back of his head was smashed out of shape and looked larger than it should have; only a few patches of red hair showed through the thick, almost black blood.

Jonathan grabbed David and looked up at him

and saw his face and where he was looking and he looked too and kept trying to say something. There, just inside the doorway, in the dimness of the hall, Mrs. Dennihan lay on her back looking up at them, in death.

Clutching at each other, they stumbled back away from the screen door and off the porch, none of them able to speak.

Then they heard Mr. Dennihan.

It was a sound like none of them had ever heard before.

A roar, such as would come from an animal, not a human being, sounded to their left near a big pine tree.

Dennihan stood there swaying back and forth, making the loud, half-animal roaring sound that at the end trailed off to a moaning cry. Then the cry started back up again with hardly a breath between. He must have been slumped over or lying in the white, powdery dirt at the base of the tree on the other side, in a stupor until they aroused him. He was covered with the dirt like flour.

He held a hatchet in his right hand. His left arm dangled from his shoulder. He had broken the cast, or ripped most of it away. Part of the cast, dirty and cracked, clung to his arm.

He roared out again and raised the hatchet and lurched toward them.

"Run!" David screamed, pushing at the others so they jumped off the side of the porch away from Dennihan. Cortland stumbled a little but ran as he stumbled until he was standing straight again and still running. Jonathan saw David grab Ellen's hand and yank her along with him.

Jonathan looked at the little hole in Ellen's bathing suit and thought about the bathing suit being hot and itchy and thought it was crazy to think about that now. Jonathan knew they probably kicked up sand on Hubert's body as they ran past him, not really looking, with Till the closest to him.

They heard Dennihan roar and moan and they could tell by the way the sound came at them that he had started after them. Jonathan saw David glance over his shoulder and then he said, "Run, oh God, run," and he sounded almost like he was crying or praying at the same time.

Dennihan must have stumbled near the steps because of the sound he made and that gave them a little more distance between them, about thirty or more yards, and then they lengthened it to fifty, but he was up and still coming after them, screaming or making some sound, not quite words.

They had to run at an angle away from Uncle Roy's house. They ran toward the creek. He was still after them.

As Dennihan ran, his roar became more of a chant, low and guttural, that pulsated with the jar of running. The distance between them was only slightly greater and Dennihan ran at a lower elevation so he was closer to the main road than they. This was having the effect of forcing them away from Uncle Roy's house.

They crossed the creek up above the swimming hole in the shallow water that looked so clear and sparking that it didn't seem right at all to Jonathan. Such pretty water was out of place with what was happening. He realized, too, for the first time that he was sobbing as he ran.

They looked ahead of them at the foot of the mountain that began to rise abruptly. Jonathan knew as soon as David that this would make it worse. Then they heard Dennihan splash into the creek, slipping around on the rocks. They glanced back and could see that Dennihan still held the hatchet and that made it harder for him every time he tried to get up.

David used the moment. "Back that way," he gasped. Dennihan was almost seventy-five yards behind them but they knew they would lose some yardage when they angled back toward the main road. There was nothing else to do. It would be too easy to trap them as they tried to make it up the little mountain.

But Dennihan was still between them and Uncle Roy's house. They only had a short strip of meadow left and then they would be at Mattaskeet Road.

Dennihan was up and cutting across the meadow, too. Jonathan knew before David spoke what they had to do.

The hill, a short sloping one with pines on each side of a clearing, lay in front of them. Beyond that, around a bend up the hill was the sled run and thickets on each side. They knew that area. There was no sense in trying to make it back to the house. They were cut off from that.

They crossed Mattaskeet Road and scurried into

the brush on the other side, beginning the run up the hill.

David yanked at Ellen, who half-stumbled as she ran. Cortland flailed his arms and legs out wildly as he ran, but he ran fast. Till ran almost as smoothly as David.

"Up there," David panted. "The sleds. Up there."

Jonathan's stomach hurt from the running, and he became conscious of the way Eureka's sharper edge bit into his hand because he clutched the rock so hard. But he didn't let it go; he held even tighter.

They had increased the distance between them and Dennihan. "A little more," David said.

Jonathan realized that with another twenty or thirty yards they could angle back slightly and be hidden from Dennihan by the smaller trees. Dennihan would be able to catch glimpses of them but they would not be completely in the open.

"To the sleds and hide," David said.

Jonathan looked at David's face and knew how hard it was for him to run and practically drag Ellen along. David's face was splotchy bright red and he kept his mouth open trying to breathe.

They could still hear Dennihan bellow, and in between, there was a half-sobbing moaning sound he made. The roar sounded almost like a word or phrase, but it was no more understandable than a bear trying to make human sounds.

Another sharp angle back toward the sled run and they were completely hidden from Dennihan. But they could hear him. The sled run was right in front of them.

"Maybe he'll think we went on straight," David said.

There at the familiar site, Jonathan felt like he had renewed breath, as they all ran swiftly and as silently as possible sharply to the left and straight up the hill they used as a sled run.

"He hasn't seen us yet," David said as he glanced back.

They came to the cistern and slowed somewhat so they could go single file around the rim of the cistern. Then they scrambled behind the tunnel of thickets that hid their sleds.

Flopping on the pine needles in the thicket, they peered out. They were trying to breathe quietly. Cortland made a noise as if he was going to vomit.

Till elbowed him sharply, "Shhh."

Cortland gulped in air and that seemed to help.

"Just in case," David said, "get the sleds ready."

Jonathan helped David with the sleds. They moved slowly and almost silently. Still hidden, the sleds were placed at the edge of the thicket, the two smaller ones lined up on the left and the large heavy one on the right. Jonathan watched David aim the big one; by moving it an inch or two, it would go just to the left of the cistern and down the hill; or ride the other side of the ridge and it would crash into the deep, rubbish-filled concrete hole.

They lay quietly. They couldn't hear Dennihan. Jonathan's right hand hurt. He looked at it and loosened his grip on Eureka. His fingers were stiff and hard to move. He flexed them and then held tightly to the rock again.

"Maybe he's given up," Cortland whispered.

But then Till breathed, "Oh, Lord, no. . . ."

Dennihan stepped through the pine trees at an angle below them.

They didn't move. Jonathan sucked in his breath and held it.

Dennihan stood down below them breathing as if his chest would cave in. His hair was matted and his shirt and trousers were wet. His face was scarlet. He gulped in air and then bellowed. He listened. No sound, then he began the moaning sobs again and his chest heaved in and out. He held the hatchet down by his side. Turning his head up to the trees he bellowed again.

Jonathan had never seen anyone's face look like that, or eyes like that.

David put his hand very softly on Ellen's back.

Dennihan took a few steps toward the cistern, paused and began to walk around it, looking to each side as he did. He was coming closer to them but did not see them.

He stopped again, moaned, looked around and came all the way around the cistern so that he stood in front of it.

Out of the corner of his eye, Jonathan saw David turn his head slowly to look once again behind where they hid, as if he hoped some opening might have occurred in the thicket and wall behind them that would let them escape that way. Jonathan felt trapped but tried to keep from crying.

Then Jonathan sensed the slight movement from David. Almost immediately, Jonathan knew what David was doing. He had moved the big sled so that it pointed to the right of the ridge, aimed so that it would go directly toward the cistern.

Then Dennihan took another half-step and stood directly in front of the cistern, no more than twenty-five yards from where they lay. Dennihan, chest heaving and legs almost buckling, slowly turned his back to their hiding place and peered into the bushes on either side.

So close and softly that Jonathan could feel the breath of his words, David whispered, "Get ready to run."

David shoved the big, heavy sled.

It went fast, whispering almost silently toward the cistern—and Dennihan.

Dennihan must have heard it or sensed it right as it approached. He wheeled around, too late.

The heavy lumber on the front of the sled smacked into Dennihan's shins and spun him backwards into the cistern with the heavy sled on top of him.

He screamed as it hit him and they heard the sled and Dennihan crash into the bottom of the cistern.

David stood up in a half-crouch. "Now! Come on . . . run! Fast! Home!"

Their only way out was past the edge of the cistern. David led the way. He pulled on Ellen's hand. Jonathan came next and then Cortland and Till in single-file.

They ran but had to slow down as they went by the cistern because it was so narrow at that point.

And that was exactly what Jonathan didn't want to do.

Dennihan had started moaning and roaring again and they could hear him scrambling around trying to get out. Then he saw them as they edged by the cistern.

Dennihan yelled, and drew back his arm to throw the hatchet. Just as he threw it, he made a heavy grunting sound as if he had been kicked in the chest, but the hatchet came anyway, spinning end over end. It caught Ellen just below the knee with a glancing blow, even as they picked up a running pace.

David kept dragging Ellen along.

Jonathan wasn't sure whether he was screaming at Dennihan and crying at the same time. But he stopped an instant and he stared right at Dennihan's distorted face. He screamed something at Dennihan.

Then he threw Eureka as hard as he could. The rock spiraled in at an absolutely straight line and struck Dennihan just forward of his left ear with a sound like hitting hard dirt with a hammer.

Even as the rock struck, it looked as if Dennihan had already begun to fall, his legs going limp under him as if that sound he had made when he threw the hatchet had been all of the life coming out of his chest. He dropped heavily to his knees, and then fell over backwards, with one foot still under him.

They ran.

They ran down the faint path the sleds had made earlier that summer and they ran through a growth of trees and across the meadow and the grape vines at its edge and they ran past the cherry tree where Jonathan had killed a bird. Ellen's leg was bleeding some. David held her hand and when they got to the edge of the yard they saw their father and mother and Uncle Roy driving up and looking startled at them. Even David was crying.

Chapter Nineteen

They sat in the kitchen and Ellen's shoulders kept shaking. Their mother warmed a heavy towel at the oven door and wrapped it around Ellen's shoulders. The cut on Ellen's leg was slight, and their mother bathed it and put medicine and a bandage on it. Cortland suddenly vomited while drinking the hot chocolate Aunt Eva had fixed.

It had been hardly anytime before the cars started driving up. By mistake the hearse came up their driveway. Then the sheriff told the drivers to go across the highway, and he stood in the side yard and pointed toward the Dennihan's pigpen house. One of the men said the easiest way to get to the cistern was from the highway, but they would have a pretty good walk. The sheriff said he did not want them to bring anything back from the cistern this way by the house, and Uncle Roy nodded.

Later on the sheriff, a tall, lanky man, came back and he stood in the driveway talking solemnly with Uncle Roy and their father. Jonathan saw them from the kitchen window. The sheriff kept turning his head to one side as he tried to light the little stub of a cigar he held in his mouth. It looked to Jonathan like he would burn his nose. Jonathan saw the almost sick look on Uncle Roy's face as the sheriff talked. Jonathan's father kept shaking his head and had his hands deep in his pockets.

Then the three of them came into the kitchen. The sheriff tried again to light his cigar by turning his head to one side.

The sheriff said, "The acting coroner, Dr. Young, has taken a look at Dennihan, and he kind of goes along with me that Dennihan probably had a heart attack about the same time he threw the hatchet—and at about the same time the rock hit him."

He tried again on his cigar. "I got to admit, though, that was a right smart job of pitching for that young fellow there. But I kind of doubt he could have throw'd it hard enough to kill that Dennihan, anyway. I figure Dennihan was already dying."

He puffed twice on the cigar and got it going. "And that's about that, as far as I figure," the sheriff said. "We'll just say that God, in his mercy, struck the man down." For the first time he took the little stub of a cigar out of his mouth, looked at it and put it back in his mouth.

Just before dark two newspaper reporters and a photographer came to the house but Uncle Roy would not let them talk to Jonathan and the others, and he would not let them take pictures. Later a picture was taken of the Dennihan's house. The wire services picked up the story and it was played, with several distortions, across the country. Years later Jonathan saw one of the stories that appeared at the time in a New York paper, trying to give the whole thing a biblical twist by having David the one throwing the rock.

That night when they got ready for bed their mother made them put on clean pajamas, and she had put clean sheets on the beds. The parents decided to let Ellen sleep in the bed with them, and then just before they were ready to get in the beds, their father and mother came into the room to talk to them. Their father said he wanted them to do the best they could to put all of it away, forever. He said he was not worried about it having any lasting bad effect on them like Aunt Eva had said it might.

He said it is not the big things that really hurt us and change us. He said it is the little things that wear away at people and that do the damage.

Jonathan knew, even then, that statement by his father was something he would remember all of his life.

During the night Jonathan woke up and heard himself crying and his father came in and got in the bed with him. Jonathan put his head on his father's shoulder and his father held him close. Jonathan could smell the cigars and perspiration on his father and feel the hair on his chest. Jonathan felt comforted and loved his father very much.

• • •

Two days later they left. They had packed up the Plymouth that Uncle Roy helped their father buy. When they were just about ready to go, Jonathan went out on the front porch by himself and looked across the meadow at the swimming hole and then up to the vacant pigpen house and on up beyond that at the tree on top of Clown Mountain. The tree was absolutely still, and with the empty house and the mountain and the tree motionless, it looked like something on a postcard.

Everyone stood in the driveway to say goodbye. Till quickly hugged David and she was crying a little as they left.

They pulled out of the driveway, and Jonathan looked up at the hill where Nobody was buried.

Then they drove away toward Raleigh and a new life, and left the silence of the mountains behind them, as much as you ever leave the mountains behind you.

ABOUT THE AUTHOR

Joseph L.S. Terrell makes his home on the Outer Banks of North Carolina, his native state, where he continues the craft of fiction-writing—with a little fishing, golfing and boating thrown in.

He may be reached through Bella Rosa Books or via email at JLSTERRELL@aol.com.

Printed in the United States
200884BV00003B/1/A